LURED BY MURDER

FISH CAMP COZY MYSTERIES, BOOK 1

SUMMER PRESCOTT

SUMMER PRESCOTT BOOKS PUBLISHING

Copyright 2024 Summer Prescott Books

All Rights Reserved. No part of this publication nor any of the information herein may be quoted from, nor reproduced, in any form, including but not limited to: printing, scanning, photocopying, or any other printed, digital, or audio formats, without prior express written consent of the copyright holder.

**This book is a work of fiction. Any similarities to persons, living or dead, places of business, or situations past or present, is completely unintentional.

CHAPTER ONE

After storming into the tiny home that she shared with her roommate and bestie, Fran, Eugenia Barkley slipped out of her shoes, kicking them into the vicinity of the shoe rack, took her hair tie out of her messy bun and shook it out, then plopped into a nearby overstuffed chair that had seen better days.

"Wow, rough day, huh?" Fran observed, pouring both of them a glass of wine and joining Eu in the living room.

"Beyond rough. I swear, if I don't get promoted to reporter and get out of the editing pool soon, I may just lose my ever-loving mind," Eu groused, staring in the general direction of the front window.

"Meh, that ship sailed a while ago," Fran remarked, drawing a mild glare from Eu, who didn't have quite enough energy for a full-on glare. "Okay, okay, tell Frannie all about it," she cooed.

"That big, important editing job Joe told me I had coming up this week, you know, the one that could've given me tons of brownie points toward getting promoted?" Eu began.

"Oh no." Fran sobered, setting her glass down on the coffee table.

"Yeah. He called me in at the end of the day, when I'd already spent hours doing the research on it to make sure it was solid, to let me know that he'd passed it on to the Editor-In-Chief's daughter. That smug little twerp wouldn't know a logical fallacy from a slippery slope." Eu made a face and took a sip of wine.

Fran's brows rose. "Little twerp? Such language coming from a lady," she said, the corner of her mouth twitching upward. Eu shot her another look. This one had more energy behind it.

"It's so frustrating. I have the credentials, but I feel like I'm continually spinning my wheels and going nowhere. The reporters who turn their stories over to me for editing would be laughed out of the business if they were published as is, but they get the bylines, and I just get the shaft if the boss wants his precious darling to have the best assignments. It's so not fair." She shook her head and gazed into her wineglass.

"So quit." Fran shrugged. "Do side gigs until you find something else."

"In L.A?" Eu snorted. "Sorry, I'm just one of those people who's very into having food and shelter. Side gigs would hold me for like a week before I starved."

Fran gazed at her; eyebrows raised.

Eu closed her eyes briefly and heaved a heavy sigh. "I'm sorry. I know I'm grouchy. I had a bad day, traffic was awful, and I worked through lunch so I'm hangry as well. How do you put up with me?"

"It ain't easy, but I can help you with one of those complaints. I kept your lasagna in the oven so it would stay warm. And, before you ask, yes, I put foil over it so it didn't dry out," Fran replied.

When Eu started to rise, Fran put a hand up to stop her.

"Just stay right there. I'll bring the dragon lady some food and the rest of the bottle of wine out here too," she said, heading to the kitchen.

"I don't deserve you," Eu called out.

"No, you don't."

"Is there garlic bread?" Eu asked hopefully, her stomach growling.

"Is there a universe that exists where lasagna comes without garlic bread?" Fran asked, carefully balancing a plate of lasagna in one hand, a tray of garlic bread in the other, with the bottle of wine tucked under her arm.

"Oh, man. This is what I needed," Eu groaned in appreciation, taking her plate from Fran, who set the tray of garlic bread in front of her on the coffee table, then topped off their wine.

"You're welcome. So, what are you going to do?" Fran asked, tucking her legs up under her on the couch.

"Same thing I always do. Suck it up, do my job, and send my resume out to any major paper that might be hiring."

"You could always come work for me." Fran gave her a sly grin.

"At the surf shop? Yeah, I'd fit in so well there, dude." Eu laughed and nearly spit out her wine.

Fran co-owned a very quirky and very popular surf shop across the street from the beach. She was pierced, tattooed, and wore board shorts and a bikini top to work most days. Her world was a far cry from the corporate treadmill upon which Eu was currently stuck.

"Seriously. It'd probably do your soul some good. Your aura has been muddied for quite a while, girl. Maybe you just need to leave those sensible pumps and pencil skirts behind and have some fun for a change. I know the boss; I could probably get more than minimum wage for you." Fran grinned.

"Tempting." Eu sighed. "Writing is fun. Gathering facts is fun. And yes, admittedly, hanging out with surfers all day long would probably be fun, but I have to keep my focus in the real world until I get on the right career path."

Fran nodded. "Yeah, I get that, but if you change your mind, come have fun. Some of us make a pretty good living that way. Got plans for tonight?" she asked, changing the subject.

"Do I ever have plans on a work night?"

"No. And you never will with that attitude. You should come out with me tonight. I'm meeting some of the guys over at Stix. It'd do you good to dance the night away."

"Thanks, but I wouldn't be much fun. I'm going to stay in, maybe soak in the tub, watch a movie." Eu shrugged.

"Wild woman. Welp, I'm gonna grab my shoes and get going. If you change your mind, just come on down." Fran put down her wineglass and bounced up from the couch, planting a kiss on the top of Eu's head on her way by.

Eu watched her walk down the hall toward her room and wished she could be so carefree. Fran breezed through life in harem pants and tank tops, her sun-streaked hair wild and free, and she never seemed to be stressed about anything.

"I can't imagine," Eu murmured, setting down her fork and washing her last bite of food down with wine.

After Fran left, Eu had another glass of wine and took it with her to the kitchen, which she predicted would be a disaster. She was correct. Fran was an amazing cook, but when she was creative in the kitchen, she left a wide path of disaster in her wake. Eu sighed. Fran was the Oscar to her Felix. She was as sloppy and lackadaisical about cleaning as Eu was fastidious.

"Well, this'll take me at least an hour. Maybe I'll get the mail first."

Bringing the mail in was another one of those tasks that Fran always seemed to forget. Eu didn't bother to put her shoes back on for the quick trip down to the mailbox, and as she was sorting through the pile on the way back to the house, she stubbed her toe on a pot of begonias that Fran had forgotten to bring in after watering them.

"Bill, bill, ad…" Eu mumbled aloud, as she hobbled back into the house.

She went to the kitchen table, which was currently teeming with lasagna-making utensils, and cleared a space so she could separate her mail from Fran's.

The last envelope at the bottom of the stack she'd retrieved had a New York return address and had been addressed to her by hand. She read the embossed label in the corner.

"Bellingham. Bellingham was her mother's maiden name…." Eu frowned and slid her finger into the corner of the envelope, tearing it open. "I regret to inform you…" Eu stopped reading aloud and swallowed past a lump that had surprisingly arisen in her throat.

She sank down into one of the ancient kitchen chairs and stared, unseeing, at the chipped vinyl plank beneath her feet. She reread the letter three times, unable to believe what it said. Shaking herself out of her reverie, Eu mechanically went through the motions of doing the dishes, lost in thought.

By the time the kitchen was sparkling, from top to bottom, Eu's day caught up with her. There would be no movie after her bath. She wouldn't stay awake long enough to watch it. Fran would be getting in late, so, dressed in her comfiest pajamas, Eu left the living room light on and headed for bed.

CHAPTER TWO

"I read your letter," Fran announced, the moment Eu walked in after work. "Why didn't you tell me about this?"

"Because I haven't seen you since I got it?" Eu said, kicking off her shoes wearily.

"Are you sad that your mom died?" Fran asked softly. "Are you okay?"

"I mean, I guess I had a moment after I read it, but I never knew her, you know? So, it's kind of like hearing that a distant relative died. Sad, but…" Eu shrugged, rubbing her temples.

"Speaking of distant relatives…" Fran continued. "That aunt of yours is a real piece of work. She didn't even try to break the news gently. She wouldn't even call herself your aunt. 'I'm your mother's sister.' What kind of horrible way is that to treat your niece?"

"From what I understand, that's pretty much how my mother was, too. Who knows? That's a segment of society I'll never be interacting with, so she just treated me like the lesser mortal that I am." Eu rolled her eyes.

"Personally, I feel like anybody who's that callous is the lesser mortal, not you. You sure you're okay?" Fran asked.

Eu sighed and slumped into a kitchen chair. "No, I'm definitely not okay, but it has nothing to do with my mother."

Fran sat across from her. "Oh, no. The boss's daughter?"

Eu nodded. "Joe called me in and asked me to correct the work she'd done so he could hand it in for publication. She'd done such an awful job that it would have taken too much time for him to do it himself."

"So, he thought he could just hand it off to you instead? When he took it away from you in the first place?" Fran asked indignantly. "The nerve!"

"Yeah, well, that's basically what I said."

"Good for you!" Fran nodded her approval.

"Hmm…don't know about that. I mean, it felt good at the time, but…"

"But what?" Fran's eyes went wide.

"But it got me fired," Eu replied, her breath coming out in a whoosh. It was hard hearing the words being said aloud. It made it real. Too real.

Fran's mouth dropped open. "Seriously?"

Eu nodded.

"Holy cow. What are you going to do?" Fran asked.

"I've been thinking about that. I thought about it the whole way home," Eu replied. "Maybe I should go take a look at the property my mother willed to me. I mean, I was shocked she did that, but if it's worth anything, maybe I could sell it and have a little nest egg until I find another job."

"You think maybe she gave you a valuable property?"

"I don't think she would own a property that wasn't valuable." Eu shrugged. "Why she gave it to me, I have no idea, but I should probably go take care of it anyway. I could do side gigs while I'm job hunting and waiting for it to sell."

Fran nodded. "Do you know anything about it at all?"

"I looked it up while I was at work, before Joe dropped his little bomb on me. It's apparently in a resort that's on a peninsula in Lake of the Ozarks. A bunch of spoiled rich people houses where their biggest worry is whether or not their boat is big enough for the parties they want to host." Eu made a face.

"Your mom was rich?" Fran asked.

"Yeah, that's what I've heard."

"Good. Then hopefully she left you a multi-million-dollar house that will keep you going until you become a famous reporter."

"It'd be nice, but I gotta say…I don't trust this," Eu admitted.

"Trust what?" Fran frowned.

"This whole thing. She never says one word to me my whole life, never bothers to even send me a birthday card, but she remembers me in her will. Seems fishy. Way fishy."

"Maybe she felt guilty about abandoning you."

"And thinks a condo on the lake will make up for it? Clearly, she never knew me."

"Her loss," Fran said gently. "So, are you really going to go out there?"

"Yeah, I think I am."

"Will you at least come out dancing with me before you go?"

"Not a chance, but I definitely will if I sell the house and become a millionaire," Eu teased.

"I'm holding you to that, girl."

CHAPTER THREE

"Hi, I'd like to rent a car. One way, please," Eu told the attendant at the kiosk in the St. Louis airport. She'd just spent over four hours stuffed into a middle seat between a large man and a plump but pleasant woman, eating only tiny bags of snacks. Getting into a car and driving through the mountains wasn't what she wanted to do, but at least there would be fresh air involved.

"Sure thing, honey. Where y'all headed?"

"It's just me, but I'm going to Lake of the Ozarks." Eu consulted the address on her phone. "Summerset Beach. Do you need the zip code?"

"Oh, dear. No, I don't need the zip code. I'm afraid I can't give you a rental," the woman said apologetically.

"What? Why?" Eu's heart skipped a beat.

"Because there would be no place out there for you to drop it off. Now, your best bet would be to either hop on a regional flight to Fort Leonard Wood, or to take a shuttle from here to there. Then, when you get there, take a taxi to Summerset Beach."

"Is this place like…out in the middle of nowhere?" Eu asked, swallowing hard.

"Of course! That's why people go there." The woman smiled.

"Which option is cheaper?" Eu asked, doing financial math in her head.

"The shuttle. There's one that stops by here a couple times a day, and the next one is due in about an hour. You could get yourself a nice meal and relax for a little bit before it comes."

At least the shuttle wasn't crowded. The hotdog that Eu had eaten at the airport in roughly four bites was sitting heavily in her nervous stomach, but the seat next to her was empty and the air conditioner was keeping the temperature cool enough to almost snow inside. Her large suitcase rode underneath the bus with everyone else's, but she stuck her laptop bag in the overhead bin, where she could keep an eye on it.

A few miles outside of St. Louis, her eyelids slid shut and didn't open again until the shuttle parked at the Fort Leonard Wood airport. After picking up her bag and tipping the driver, Eu opened an app on her phone and requested a ride to the address her aunt had given her in Summerset Beach. The next available car wouldn't arrive for half an hour, so she had time to go into the airport and freshen up a bit. After brushing her teeth with a disposable toothbrush and wiping away the dark circles that had appeared under her eyes as her eyeliner melted in the heat and humidity of the early fall Missouri day, she made her way back to the meetup point for her ride.

Her bearded driver wore a plaid shirt and kept his hair a bit on the longer side, but he was wonderfully polite, helping her with her bags and offering her a bottle of water. As they drove out of the airport, Eu realized they had driven into a place that was like another world.

"Wow, it's so beautiful," she breathed.

"Yes, ma'am, it sure is," the driver agreed. "And it's only gonna get better the closer we get to the lake."

"Oh, my gosh, is that actually an eagle?" Eu exclaimed, craning her neck to watch the regal bird as it flew overhead.

"Probably. We see 'em all the time up here. Where y'all from?"

"L.A," Eu replied.

The driver glanced in the rearview mirror and grinned. "First time out here?"

"Yep, first time."

"Well now, you're in for a treat."

They were quiet for the rest of the trip, with Eu drinking in the beautiful scenery. When they came around a bend, she caught her first glimpse of the massive lake and gasped.

"Holy cow!" she whispered.

"Beautiful, ain't it? We're almost there now," the driver announced.

The road he took was steep and winding, and Eu had to yawn to clear her ears more than once as the altitude rose. When he turned onto a dirt road and headed closer to the lake, she sat up straight.

"Ummm…are we going the right way?" she asked.

"Yes, ma'am, see the sign?" He pointed to a carved wooden sign that read: Paradise Pointe.

"So, we're here?"

"Just about."

The road into the community passed an adorable general store, a pool with a huge log-cabin style clubhouse, and marinas on both sides of the road. When structures started appearing, Eu saw an old-fashioned playground, with cabins lining the peninsula. The slat-sided cabins appeared to be in good shape, but very…normal, and not at all what she expected from her mother.

"Cabins?" she murmured.

"Here we are, number 17," the driver announced.

Keys had been mailed along with the explanation letter and the deed that had Eu's name on it, so while the driver gathered her bags, Eu went to the cabin and unlocked the door. When she stepped inside, she couldn't have been more amazed.

There was a Gone Fishin' sign on the front door, and the interior was decorated in what looked like an upscale fishing theme. There was a wooden piece of art with a bear in a canoe holding a fishing pole that said, 'My Happy Place' on the bottom of it, prominently displayed on the wall in the foyer, and the colors in the living room and foyer were done in shades of sage green and warm beige. The furniture was clearly expensive, but looked comfortable, and the view was spectacular.

The cabin was a short walk away from the water's edge and had its own dock. A spacious deck overlooking the water beckoned from behind a set of French doors in the living room.

"Wow, this is beautiful," the driver said, startling her.

She smiled and tipped him, insisting that he didn't need to take her suitcase beyond the foyer. After he was gone, she took her time exploring the cabin. Her cabin. The floors were wide-planked wood in all of the main areas, with thick, neutral colored carpet in the three bedrooms. The main suite had a king-sized bed that faced floor-to-ceiling windows with a lake view. Every room was stocked with necessities, fluffy towels, blankets, extra pillows, games, and a small library. Eu discovered, much to her delight, that the bathrooms and kitchen had all the necessities as well, except for food.

"This definitely doesn't track with what I know about my mother, but if I'm going to be here until I can put it up for sale, I might as well get settled in."

CHAPTER FOUR

After lugging her suitcase and laptop bag into the main bedroom and stashing her clothes in the oddly fresh-smelling closet and dresser, Eu decided to change into a pair of rugged-looking cargo shorts that had been a gift from Fran, along with the slightly worn polo shirt that she typically donned on the days when she deep-cleaned the house. They were the only items she had that would come close to passing for camping gear, and from the glimpses she'd caught of the community on the way to her cabin, there was a distinctly camp-like vibe to the area.

"A walk to clear my head would probably do me some good," she murmured, looking forward to inhaling the fresh, pine-scented air. Making a quick plan to head down to the general store to check out their food selections, she pocketed her key and closed the door behind her.

Standing on the immaculate 'A Bad Day Fishing is Better Than a Good Day Working' mat in front of the door, Eu looked to the left and saw a locked shed that had been built so seamlessly into the exterior of the cabin that she hadn't even spotted it on her way in.

"That must be what one of those other keys on my keyring is for," she mused, digging the keys out of her pocket and heading to the shed.

One of the keys fit into the lock and when she opened the shed door, Eu was surprised by the contents of the small space.

"Pool floaties and fishing gear?" Her brows rose and she stepped into the shed, feeling a bit like Alice must've felt when she plopped down into Wonderland.

There were folding nylon camping chairs in tidy tubes, hanging on the wall next to the pool noodles and inflatable mats, a tackle box filled with tackle, and a single fishing pole that looked used, but very well cared for.

"This is the first outdoor shed I've ever seen that didn't have cobwebs."

As she gazed at the high-quality fishing pole neatly clipped to an organizing rack, an overwhelming wave of nostalgia swept through her. "Dad would've said this one was a beauty," she whispered, running her fingers lightly over the cool surface of the pole. She stared at it, tracing her fingers over the brand name that even a greenhorn would recognize, when inspiration struck. "When in Rome," she murmured, opening the lid to the tackle box, her eyes roving over the bits and pieces of necessary fishing items she'd forgotten existed. She assessed what she might need to take down to the water and go fishing, then headed for the general store, hoping they'd have bait.

A cluster of sleigh bells jangled when Eu opened the glass door of the general store, announcing her arrival. There was a tattooed, stick-thin older woman in a baggy tank top behind the counter reading a magazine, and when she looked up and saw Eu, her face paled as though she'd seen a ghost, and the magazine slipped from her hand.

"Hi!" Eu said, her overly bright tone sounding as phony as it felt. She was alone in a place where she knew no one and wanted to go fishing in waters that she'd never fished. It was intimidating to say the least, but then again, she'd pretty much walk through fire to bring back the sweet memories of when her dad used to take her fishing. "Uh, is everything okay?" she asked, when the woman continued to stare at her.

"I'm still breathin'," the woman replied, seeming to shake off whatever had been bothering her. "What can I do ya fer?" she asked, her accent as thick as honey, her voice as rough as sandpaper.

"Well, I just arrived today, so I'm going to need some groceries, and then I saw on your sign that you have bait, so I'll get the bait now and the groceries later, I guess," Eu babbled on as the woman nodded.

"Good enough. How many you need?" the woman asked, coming out from behind the counter.

"I'm sorry…how many what?" Eu asked.

"Minnows." The woman looked at her curiously.

"Umm…wait…minnows? I was thinking like maybe those stinky marshmallows, or some of the glow in the dark salmon eggs or something non-alive like that," Eu said, remembering that anytime they'd used nightcrawlers to fish, her dad had baited her hook. Even in college.

The cashier grinned. "Well, what is it you're wantin' to catch?" she asked, looking as though she was trying not to laugh.

"You know, I have no idea what kind of fishing you do out here. I'm not from here, as you might have guessed." Eu could feel herself blushing. Her impulsive decision to go fishing might have been a mistake, but she so wanted to now.

"I could tell that right off." The woman nodded. "You're related to Randi, aintcha?" she asked, looking at Eu closely.

"I'm sorry, who?" Eu frowned.

"Pretty lil thing from New York. Rich girl. Had hair and eyes just like yours."

Eu's stomach did a little flip, and her hand went to her wavy mahogany hair. She cleared her throat, unable to speak for a moment. "Umm…by Randi, do you mean Miranda? Miranda Bellingham?" she asked, her throat closing and making the last syllable squeak.

"Yep, that's her. She's good people. Ain't seen her in a while, but I couldn't miss the resemblance when you walked in. She looked just like that back in the 80s. How's she doing?"

"She, uh…she passed, recently," Eu replied, taking a deep breath.

"Oh, no. I'm so sorry. She was lookin' a lil sickly last time I saw her now that I think of it." The woman nodded. "I'm sorry, hon. You her little girl?"

Eu nodded. "Yeah, I guess I am."

"I'm Trixie. I own this fine establishment." She stuck out a gnarled hand and Eu shook it.

"Thanks, I'm Eu. Nice to meet you."

"Beg pardon?"

"I said, nice to meet you," Eu repeated.

"No, before that. You said you were me…" Trixie said, frowning.

"Oh, no, that's not… My name is Eugenia, and I've always hated it, so everyone calls me Eu."

Trixie chuckled, a raspy smoker's laugh. "Another rich girl name. Miranda preferred Randi too. Now that we know each other, lemme get you set up. Your mama loved to fish, so I bet you'll be good at it," she said, leading Eu toward a giant aquarium where thousands of minnows darted back and forth.

My mother fished???

"I hope so. It's been a long time."

"Now, what most folks love to catch 'round these parts is crappie, because they're good eatin' and they put up a nice fight. Crappie like minnows, so I'll set you up with a couple dozen to get you started," Trixie said, reaching for a small net that was hanging by the aquarium. "These ones are nice and lively, so you should be able to catch somethin'."

"Oh…well, I…I've never actually fished with minnow," Eu admitted.

"Okay, well the first thing that you'll need to know is how to put 'em on the hook. Lemme show ya." Trixie dipped a small, Styrofoam bucket into the minnow water, then captured several nets full of the wriggling little fishes and deposited them in the bucket. When she was finished, she stuck her hand down into the water and grabbed a minnow, then held it up for Eu to see. "So, you open his mouth with the business end of the hook, then you thread it through the gill real careful so you don't poke him." She stuck a fingernail between the fish's lips, and it opened its mouth.

"Oh, that's great! So, he won't feel any pain or bleed or anything?" Eu let out a breath.

Trixie stared at her for a moment. "Not yet. Honey, this critter is gonna get swallowed by a giant at some point. I don't think you need to worry about his welfare. It's the circle of life. The crappie eats him, and you eat the crappie."

Eu swallowed hard and nodded. She didn't really like thinking about the circle of life when it came to her food. "But…you said 'yet'. Is there something more aggressive I have to do to him before the fish bites him?"

"Well…yeah. If you just thread the hook through the gill and leave it like that, he'll wiggle right off. So, after the hook goes through the gill, you rotate it toward the backbone and push it through, so that the tip comes out the other side of him." She pantomimed the action.

"I don't know if I can do that," Eu admitted.

Trixie shrugged. "Your mama could."

Challenge accepted. If my mother could do it…

"Fine, then. I'll make it happen."

Trixie gave her a puzzled look. "Good. Now, if you want to catch sunfish, you can use worms…" she began.

Eu shook her head and shuddered. "I don't know what sunfish are, but I won't be needing any worms."

"I bet." Trixie chuckled. "Now, catfish will eat just about anything, so use what you want for those. The stink bait and marshmallows are over there." She inclined her head toward the register after dropping the minnow back into the Styrofoam bucket and dried her hands on a towel hanging by the aquarium. "There's a covered fishin' hole on the marina docks at the opposite side of the peninsula from your cabin." She pointed across the parking lot. "It's got lighting if you wanna go night fishin' and there's places for your tackle, but you can fish from any of the docks in both marinas. You got a license?"

"Oh, no! I forgot you need a license to fish. I guess I'll have to give you these back," Eu said, holding up the bucket of minnows.

"No, you won't. Just go online and you can get a fishin' license right away. You'll want to take a couple of bottles of water with you when you head out, too."

"Why?" Eu asked, distracted by the thought of baiting her own hook.

"…to drink?" Trixie said, giving her a look.

"Oh, yeah. Of course. I'll take a candy bar, too."

When Eu walked back to the cabin to get her chair and fishing tackle, she could hear the water sloshing inside her bucket of minnows. "First time for everything," she muttered.

CHAPTER FIVE

"I'm a self-sufficient woman who can do whatever I put my mind to," Eu mumbled Fran's mantra aloud while slinging a camp chair over her shoulder and trying to juggle a small cooler, her fishing pole, tackle box, and the minnow bucket.

She located a sign across the parking lot that said, 'Fishin' Hole' and had an arrow pointing to a path that wound its way between two cabins, down to the marina. There was a small footbridge which led from the land to the docks where cabin owners parked their boats, and at the far end of the dock, Eu spotted a simple structure that had to be the fishing hole.

She discovered the fishing hole was literally that; a rectangular opening in the plywood floor of a wooden shack that had been built on the dock. The hole itself, which had two-foot-high rails around it, looked to be roughly five feet wide by seven feet long. From the edges of the hole to the sides of the shack, there was a six foot border for chairs, tackle, and whatever else was needed in the fishing process. Large shutters that would cover glassless windows in the winter were now held open for airflow by metal hook-and-eye fasteners.

There were two people sitting in camp chairs at the hole when Eu entered, dodging a giant spider web that had been spun from one side of the doorframe to the other. The man at the five-foot side of the hole had wavy dark hair that was silvering at the temples. He was so handsome that he seemed out of place in his surroundings. He appeared to be reading something on his phone, while his fishing pole dangled in his other hand, but he looked up and smiled when Eu set her tackle box down across from him.

The shack's other occupant was a heavy-set woman with hair that looked like it hadn't seen a brush in quite some time. She wore drab olive-green sweatpants, a t-shirt that had seen better days, and ancient tennis shoes that were literally reinforced with duct tape. She glanced up when Eu entered, but her expression was far from welcoming.

The hot guy stood and stashed his phone in his pocket, moving close enough to the corner to introduce himself while still keeping his line in the same spot.

"You're a new face around here," he observed. "I'm Michael."

Eu shook his extended hand. "Nice to meet you. I'm Eu...uh Eugenia, but everyone calls me Eu," she amended.

"That's not confusing at all," he teased, his dark eyes sparkling.

"Right?" Eu laughed. "Hi, there!" she called out to the woman sitting almost directly across from her on Michael's left. "I'm Eugenia...and you are...?"

"Fishing," the woman grunted, giving her a dirty look.

Eu glanced at Michael, who rolled his eyes.

"So, tell me, Eu, are you familiar with fishing here?" he asked.

"No. This is the first time I've held a fishing pole in literally decades, and the last time I fished with my dad, it was for trout in Idaho."

"Okay, well this is very different, but easy once you get the hang of it. Are you familiar with using minnows as bait?"

"Trixie filled me in on it when I bought them," Eu said with a grimace.

"Okay, good. It's not as awful as it seems. I can help you figure it out if you have questions. Basically, put a weight on your line, use crappie hooks, and when you're ready to put your line in the water, just release it and let it drop down for about twelve seconds. If you drop it lower than that you run the risk of getting a catfish, if you leave it closer to the surface, you might get a sunfish. There's also a tree branch right here." He pointed to the corner between them. "You'll want to stay away from that so your line doesn't get snagged."

"Okay, that makes sense," Eu said, relaxing a bit.

"And if you're really lucky, you might snag a bass on occasion," Michael added.

"Ohhh…that sounds delicious." Eu grinned.

As she tied on her hook, and attached her split weights to the line, memories of a much simpler time in her life flooded in. She and her dad had the best talks about everything and nothing while they sat, poles in hand, perfectly content.

Once her line was ready, Eu looked down at the minnow bucket with trepidation. "I can do this," she said under her breath, plunging her hand down into the cool water in the bucket and grabbing a minnow. "I'm sorry little buddy," she whispered, carefully threading the hook through the squiggling critter's mouth and out of its gill.

When it came time to thread it through the back, however, the thought made her queasy, so she made a split-second decision to just put the minnow in the water in its current state. As soon as she dangled her hook above the water's surface, the minnow flipped, flopped, and leaped his way to freedom, darting into the depths in a silvery flash.

The older woman across the way glared at her and shook her head.

"Here, let me show you a quick and easy way to do that," Michael offered, leaning his pole against the railing and dipping his hand into the bucket for a minnow. "See, you thread it through, just like you did," he said, grabbing her empty hook and doing what she'd done. "Then, you put the tip of the hook right here, below its dorsal fin, then gently push it through. Think of it like ear piercing. Hurts at first, but then it's fine." He demonstrated the technique. "See, he can still swim in a normal position – that's why it's so effective."

"Thank you," Eu replied, feeling oddly relieved by his explanation.

She dropped her line into the water and eased down into her camp chair. The moment she got herself settled; the tip of her pole bounced with a bite.

"Oh, holy moly!" Eu said, setting the hook and leaping to her feet to reel the fish in.

"Okay, wait now," Michael cautioned. "If it's as big as it seems it might be, you shouldn't lift it up over the rail. It might flop off the line. Let me grab a net and help you," he offered.

Eu reeled until she could see the large crappie right below the surface. Michael stood beside her and netted the fish perfectly, bringing it up onto the deck around the fishing hole.

From that point on, it was like riding a bicycle. Muscle memory took over and she handled the sizable crappie like a pro. Grabbing the fish by the lower jaw with her thumb and forefinger, she dislodged her hook, surprised to see that her minnow was still on it, then lifted it up to the measuring stick to check the length. It was definitely a keeper.

"Way to go! Do you have a basket or a stringer to keep it in or on?" Michael asked.

"Shoot. I guess I wasn't thinking that far ahead," Eu admitted, feeling utterly inept.

"No worries. I have an extra in my boat you can use. I'll run and get it if you'll keep an eye on my line."

"Of course. Thank you so much," Eu replied, hating the fact that she kept looking like a damsel in distress in front of the hot guy. *Then again, if one must be rescued, it isn't awful to have a handsome rescuer…*

"My pleasure." Michael carefully took the fish from her and headed over to where the boats were docked.

Eu held Michael's pole in one hand and examined her other hand. There was a sprinkle of tiny scales from the minnow on her finger, and a trace of a substance she couldn't quite identify under her thumbnail.

"Gross. This is fun, but it's going to destroy my manicure," she observed.

The older woman gazed up at her with an expression of what looked like disgust.

"Sorry, I didn't realize I'd said that aloud." Eu attempted a chuckle, but when the woman's expression didn't change, she gave up on the pretense.

Michael reappeared with her fish in a basket, and lowered it into the water to her left, securing it to the railing. She was about to hand his pole over when the tip of it suddenly bent, the line veering sharply to the left.

"Oh, my goodness, you have a huge bite," she yelped, but when she tried to reel in, the line wasn't even taut.

Michael peered over the railing. "Nah, that's just Leonardo messing around," he said with a shrug. "Don't reel it in, you might hook him."

Eu stopped reeling and stared at Michael. "Leonardo?"

"Yeah, look." He pointed into the water and Eu saw a turtle lazily paddling around in the water. "When he passes too close to the line, sometimes it gets stuck on his shell. He hangs out here, hoping to score some minnow fragments after we pull in a fish."

"Quite a ninja, huh?" Eu quipped.

"Exactly." Michael chuckled.

The afternoon passed quickly, with Eu catching several more fish. As she packed up her things, preparing to head back up to the cabin, Michael asked if she knew how to clean them.

"It's been a long time, but I know how," she replied, her mind going back to lakeside lessons given by her dad.

"Always be thankful for the gift of nourishment, Eu. That's no small thing," he'd said, always pausing for a moment in reverent silence before beginning to clean their catch.

"Should I bring the basket back here or drop it off at your cabin when I'm done with it?" Eu asked, shaking off the melancholy that came with missing her dad.

"Doesn't matter to me," he said. "I'm number 13. You can leave it on the porch if that's easier."

"Great, thanks again. Have a good rest of the day," Eu replied, shouldering her chair and grabbing all her items, including the basket of flopping fish.

"You, too. Need help with any of that?" Michael asked.

"Nah, I'm good."

Eu trudged back toward her cabin, and as soon as she stepped off of the foot bridge and onto land, a snake rippled across the path in front of her.

Unable to stifle a blood-curdling scream, she made a madcap run to the top of the hill, minnows sloshing and fish flopping as she went. Huffing, puffing, and embarrassed, she looked back toward the fishing hole and saw Michael standing in the doorway, watching her, with his hands in his pockets and a grin on his face. Pretending she hadn't seen him, she marched over the crest of the hill and across the parking lot, her face aflame.

CHAPTER SIX

Eu woke up to the sweet sound of birds chirping outside her window but was entirely disoriented for a moment when she opened her eyes and wasn't in her bedroom in Los Angeles. Then she glanced over to the wall of windows overlooking the lake and smiled.

"I haven't slept that hard in a while," she marveled, sitting up and stretching her arms over her head. "Must be the fresh air. I can't wait to sit out on the dock and have my coffee." A horrible thought crossed her mind as soon as the words left her lips. She had no coffee.

"Desperate times call for desperate measures." She sighed, tossed the covers back, and slid her legs over the side of the bed. A trip to the general store wasn't high on her list of activities to do first thing in the morning, but she had to have her coffee. The sooner the better.

Not caring how she might look, since the atmosphere at the resort was so wonderfully informal, Eu slipped into a pair of denim shorts, donned a baggy sweatshirt, and secured her hair up into a messy bun. Her flip flops waited for her at the front door and after wriggling her toes into them, she headed for the general store, credit card in hand.

The walk to the store was uphill, and by the time she was halfway there, her thighs were burning in protest. She passed by the older woman from the fishing hole, who was sitting on her front porch, smoking a pipe.

"Good morning," Eu called out, waving with far more enthusiasm than she actually felt. Of course, the woman merely stared at her with a vague look of disapproval, puffing her pipe and not saying a word.

Not even close to ready to deal with that kind of negativity so early in the day, Eu continued on, trying not to huff and puff, as she hiked up the hill to the general store. Much to her horror, when Eu finally approached the rustic little store, the lights were off, and the door was locked.

She read the sign. Off season hours: 8-4 Monday thru Saturday. Eu pulled her phone from the back pocket of her shorts and checked the time.

"It's only 6:45?" she muttered, peering through the glass door to make certain that Trixie wasn't lurking near the register reading a magazine. "Of course not." Eu sighed. She started back down the hill, seriously considering going back to bed so that she could sleep until the store opened.

When she reached cabin 13, Michael came out onto his porch. "Looking for this?" he asked, holding up a mug that had steam curling over its rim. Eu hurried over and smelled the freshly brewed coffee even before he handed it to her.

"Is it that obvious?" she asked, running a hand over her untamed mane, acutely aware of her poor choice of outfit.

"Not at all. It just didn't look like you were out for a casual morning walk when I saw you go up the hill. Trixie isn't a morning person. She charges more for bait during the season just because she has to get up earlier for the fishermen." Michael chuckled. "Cream? Sugar?" he asked, pointing at her mug.

"Both, please," Eu replied, greatly relieved that she didn't have to wait until eight o'clock for her caffeine fix. He took the mug from her.

"I'll be back in a minute. Have a seat." He motioned to a pair of rocking chairs on the porch that looked like they'd been constructed from the trunks of small trees.

Eu thanked him profusely when he handed her back her mug of coffee. It was exactly the right color and had just a light touch of sweetness. Perfection.

"You make a mean cup of coffee," Eu said, relishing another sip.

"Thanks. I'm a bit of a coffee snob. I bring a trunk of it with me every time I come here, and I grind my own beans," Michael replied.

"I did that at home," Eu confessed. "Out here, I'm guessing I'll have to rough it." She chuckled.

"I can give you a bag of freshly ground until you can get to the grocery store. It'll make roughing it a bit more palatable."

"You're a saint." Eu grinned.

"Nah, not a saint, just a boy scout." Michael shrugged.

Eu gazed over at the cabin that sat kitty-corner to Michael's, where the glowering woman had sat smoking her pipe a few minutes earlier.

"Who's she and why does she instantly hate me?" she asked, inclining her head toward the cabin.

"That's Crappie Callie. She's the only resident who stays in the complex year round. I don't think she hates you specifically, I think she just distrusts new people in general."

"Why?" Eu asked.

"Who knows? She plays her cards pretty close to the vest. I've been coming here for decades, and she still only nods at me for a greeting. Maybe she just wants to keep all the fish for herself." Michael chuckled. "She's a pretty legendary fisherperson, you know."

"Must've made her madder than a hatter when I caught some yesterday, then." Eu grinned.

"Oh, I think that ship sailed a long time ago."

"Does she live by herself?" Eu asked.

"As far as I know. I've never seen anyone else at her cabin."

"Maybe that's why she's so sour. Loneliness can do awful things to a person, I'd guess," Eu murmured, staring in the direction of Callie's cabin.

"Maybe so."

"What's it like during the winter here? Why doesn't anyone other than Callie stay?"

"Well, once the tourists are gone, most of the businesses around here shut down for the off-season, and the ones that do stay open are closed anytime there's snow or ice. I'm guessing that probably has a lot to do with it."

"Oh, wow, it snows and gets icy here?" The very thought made Eu cold. This seventy degree morning was about as cold as she was willing to tolerate. She may have grown up in Idaho, but she'd been a southern Californian for quite a while.

"Not usually too badly, from what I understand, but bad enough to shut down all businesses and services."

Eu shivered involuntarily and wrapped her hands around her coffee mug, as if trying to absorb the warmth in advance.

"So, I'm guessing, based upon the limited supply of actual food that Trixie sells, you probably don't have anything for breakfast either, right?" Michael asked.

"I mean…I have a candy bar, if that counts. But don't worry, I'll be fine," Eu assured him.

"That's a shame, because I have a warm batch of homemade cinnamon rolls and I'd never be able to eat them all myself. Maybe Callie is hungry," Michael mused with a sly grin.

"You have homemade cinnamon rolls?" Eu's mouth watered. Her stomach growled audibly, and she blushed.

"Well, since your stomach seems to have just protested your decision to remain hungry, how about I go grab a couple for us?" Michael asked, rising from his chair.

They chatted while they ate, about everything and nothing, and time flew.

"Now that I'm stuffed and sleepy, I guess it's time to go home and make myself presentable for a trip to the grocery store," Eu said. "Thank you so much for breakfast. I can't remember the last time I had fresh, warm cinnamon rolls. Those things could be habit forming."

"Absolutely, my pleasure. I'm glad you enjoyed them. Do you have a way to get to the grocery store?"

"I was thinking about taking an Uber."

Michael stared at her for a moment. "You didn't google how far away it was, did you?" he asked.

Eu sighed. "No. I'm guessing the charge would be more than my grocery bill?"

"Likely." Michael nodded. "I'd be happy to give you a ride."

"I wouldn't want to impose," Eu said, hating the feeling of helplessness that had engulfed her. She didn't have unlimited funds to spend on Uber rides, but she didn't want to take advantage of a stranger's kindness either.

"No imposition at all. I have to pick up a few things for my chicken piccata anyway." Michael shrugged.

I love chicken piccata. This gorgeous man cooks.

"Oh! Well then, if it's no trouble."

"No trouble at all. Just drop by whenever you're ready. I don't exactly have a tight schedule when I'm out here."

His grin was a joy to behold. Someone that good looking couldn't possibly be this sweet…could he?

CHAPTER SEVEN

Michael helped Eu bring in the groceries, setting bags on the counter in her kitchen and going out for more loads.

"You have a ton of cucumbers in these bags," he remarked.

"They were on sale. Besides, I love making pickles, and fermented foods are very healthy," Eu shrugged.

Fran had once said that she would walk through fire for a jar of Eu's homemade pickles. Eu always made extra jars because Fran would occasionally just eat a jar of pickles for a meal.

"I'm a fan of pickles," Michael said. "So that's good to know. Your place is beautiful," he observed, glancing about.

"Oh, thanks. Only the best for my mother. At least her insistence upon nice things should make it sell pretty quickly."

"Wow, you're going to sell? This cabin is one of the best properties in the complex. Mine isn't quite as nice as this one and I wouldn't sell for anything, even though I'm only here a few months out of the year."

"Well, I need some funds so I can figure out what to do with my life, so it seems like selling is the way to go. What do you do that allows you to be here for months at a time?" Eu asked, changing the subject.

"I'm a professor at a university in Illinois."

"Oh? That's great! What do you teach?" It was shameless of her, but Eu had learned from experience that the way to avoid difficult conversations was to ask people about themselves. At least in this instance, she really was interested in what Michael had to say.

"Physics."

"You and I would never have been on the same side of campus when I was a student."

"You're assuming I was teaching when you were a student?" Michael grinned and arched an eyebrow at her.

Eu felt her face flush with embarrassment.

"Well, I didn't mean to assume but... weren't you?" she asked, turning to put groceries away so he couldn't see her color deepen.

"Probably." He chuckled. "Let's see, I'm guessing you're in your late twenties, which means I would've been teaching when you were in college."

"Early thirties, but who's counting?"

"I've always been a proponent of celebrating birthdays without disclosing the year, so it's all good. Anyway, I'm going to go put my groceries away now. Let me know if you forgot anything. My pantry is pretty well stocked."

"Thanks again," Eu called out as Michael headed for the door.

"Anytime," was the cheery reply.

He couldn't be more than six or seven years older than her. Not that it mattered.

Eu washed the copious amounts of cucumbers that she'd picked up and started slicing them into thin, evenly sized rounds, thankful for the razor-sharp knives she'd found in the knife block by the stove. She couldn't help but wonder who did the things like cooking and laundry and other chores that her mother likely entrusted to household help when Miranda was staying at the cabin.

"I can't even imagine her being here," she murmured, slicing repeatedly.

Once the cucumbers were sliced, she packed them into the waiting jars she'd bought at the grocery store and put vinegar, sugar, pickling spices, and salt into a large pot to boil. The smell of pickle juice began to permeate the cabin's interior, so she opened the sliders that led to the deck and pulled the screen across to keep the bugs away.

Eu was at the stove, stirring the bubbling juice when a loud knock at the door startled her. Frowning, and irritated that her pulse leapt a bit at the thought that it might be Michael on the other side of the door, she wiped her hands on a kitchen towel and headed to the foyer.

"Hey, there!" a brassy blonde woman with heavily penciled eyebrows and eyelashes like batwings greeted her. She looked absurdly out of place in her Chanel knockoff suit, kitten heels, and bright pink lipstick. "How are ya? I'm Sue-Lynn Matlock, the realtor who floats your boat," the woman said, handing her a card. "And honey, what on earth is that smell?"

She had a raspy voice that made her sound like a southern version of Demi Moore.

"Oh, sorry. I'm making pickles. I love the smell of the juice when it's cooking, so I hardly notice it. Was there something you needed?" Eu asked, glad she'd turned the juice down to low before answering the door. Pickle juice bubbling in the pan was fantastic. Pickle juice bubbling over onto the stove and turning into acrid cement was a nightmare.

"Well, I just love pickles. Anyhoo, I decided to drop by because I heard about your unfortunate situation. Please accept my humblest condolences. I thought, with things being how they are, that you might be interested in selling this property. I'm the top realtor in all of Loto, so I thought I might be able to help."

"Uh, thanks. Loto?" Eu asked, darting a glance back toward the kitchen.

The realtor stared at her for a moment, then let out a fake laugh. "Yes, Loto. Lake of the Ozarks. It's quicker than saying all those syllables."

"Ah, gotcha. Well, listen, I'm actually glad you came by. I'd love to have that conversation with you regarding selling, but now isn't a good time, since my pickles are needing attention," Eu began.

"Oh! Say no more, hon," Sue-Lynn interrupted. "You just give me a call when you're ready, and if I'm in the area before you call, I'll just drop by to check in. You go on and finish those pickles now," she said, pasting on a smile and heading back to her car before Eu could reply.

"Please don't drop by to check in." Eu sighed and closed the door.

She focused on pickle-making for the next couple of hours, then, when the jars were all stashed away, decided that it would be a smart idea to look online for a side job while she got everything prepared to sell the cabin. She had to search on her phone, since apparently her mother hadn't set up internet.

"Sweet, I think I'd be a good fit for both these jobs," Eu said, hitting the 'Apply Now' button to send her resume. "Then, once this place sells, I'll have to figure out what to do with my life."

Remembering that Michael had said he loved pickles, Eu found some twine in a drawer and made makeshift bows with it for two of the jars. Then, determined to make friends with Crappie Callie whether the older woman wanted her to or not, she did the same with two more jars. "I'm going to make you like me and be social," she vowed. "You'll get one dill and one bread and butter, just like Michael. You won't be able to resist them." She grinned triumphantly, congratulating herself on being the bigger person.

She stopped at Michael's cabin first, hoping he'd answer the door and affirm that giving Callie some pickles was a good idea, but when he didn't appear, she simply left his jars on the welcome mat and headed for Callie's cabin. Thankfully, Callie didn't answer the door either, so she left the pickles and scurried away before the old woman spotted her and opened the door to rain down verbal abuse.

"It's been a good day," she said to no one in particular as she trotted back down the hill to her cabin. "I've gone grocery shopping, made pickles, met a realtor, applied for a couple of online gigs, and reached out to an old hermit. I think it's time to go fishing. Might as well stock up in case the cabin doesn't sell as fast as I'd like it to."

As she walked down to the fishing hole, pole over her shoulder and a spring in her step, Eu took deep breaths, filling her lungs with fresh air, and enjoying the sunshine on her face.

"A girl could definitely get used to this."

CHAPTER EIGHT

Neither Michael nor Crappie Callie were at the fishing hole when Eu arrived, so she had plenty of solitude, which she spent catching fish after fish. Rather than cleaning and filleting her catch on her own dock, she decided to use the sink and cleaning board at the marina, stashing her bounty in one of the clean plastic bags that she'd kept in her tackle box.

The sun was beginning to slip toward the horizon as she made her way back to the cabin, keeping a sharp eye out for snakes on the path. She hadn't yet encountered any after the first one, but she wasn't going to let her guard down.

As Eu got closer to her porch, she saw two jars of pickles sitting on it. With them was a piece of paper with handwriting on it that looked like it belonged to a kindergartener who'd had too much caffeine. *I don't take no charity.*

"Wow," she commented, shaking her head. "Your loss, lady. My pickles are pretty epic, if I do say so myself." Her hands were full, so she left the jars where they sat for a moment, eager to get her catch into the house where she could wash it one more time before bagging it up and freezing it.

When Eu set the plastic bag of filets in the sink, a sudden movement caught her eye. She looked up, her heart pounding in her chest, and saw a shadow move on the porch. She flipped on the porch light and grabbed a broom, the first thing she could think of to ward off harm. She ran toward the porch brandishing it and saw Sue-Lynn Matlock staring at her as though she'd gone mad.

Eu went to the sliding door and hurled it open. "What are you doing here and how did you get in?" she demanded, adrenaline surging through her.

"Well, my goodness, there's no need to get your tailfeathers in an uproar. There was a key under the rock out front. I just wanted to scope out the view so I could talk about it in your listing." Sue-Lynn's lashes fluttered, as if to proclaim her innocence.

"I'm sorry, but I don't care if there was a key there or not, it was absolutely not okay for you to use it. Now hand it over and see yourself out," Eu demanded, holding her hand out for the key.

Sue-Lynn's lipsticked mouth puffed into a pout that would've done any truculent five-year-old proud, and she slapped the key into Eu's palm. "Help me help you, you know what I mean?" she muttered as she passed Eu on her way to the door.

Shaking her head, Eu went to the sink, rinsed off the filets and stored them properly in the freezer before lighting the grill so she could cook the chicken thighs that had been marinating in a teriyaki/lime/ginger mixture in the refrigerator.

She'd just placed the chicken on the grill when she heard a cheery hello from below the deck. When she looked down, Michael waved up at her.

"Hey, neighbor. Thanks for the pickles. I brought you something." He held up a brown paper bag.

"Oh, you're welcome! Meet me at the front door." Eu pointed and Michael nodded, heading for the front of the cabin.

Eu opened the door and glanced down, remembering the jars of pickles that Callie had left on her porch. She smiled when she saw them missing. Clearly Callie had changed her mind, and once she tasted those pickles, Eu was quite sure she'd be a whole lot kinder.

"You didn't have to bring me anything," she protested when Michael handed her the bag.

"Of course I didn't, but it's not like I can eat two loaves of freshly baked French bread all by myself, so here you go. It's still warm."

"I'll make pickles every week if you keep bringing out the fresh baked goods. I love cooking, but I can't bake to save my life. Thanks for this."

"You're most welcome. I saw Sue-Lynn sniffing around here earlier. Did you list your cabin with her?" Michael asked.

"No, and after what she pulled today, I probably won't."

"Oh, no. What happened?"

Eu related the incident, and he shook his head.

"That's some nerve," he commented. "She's pushy, for sure, but they say she's the best."

"Well, then maybe I'll just have to settle for second best. I don't think I can work with someone who has already broken my trust in such a major way. She scared the daylights out of me. I thought she was a burglar or something."

"Not too many burglars in these parts, but I can see how that would've been jarring. Hey, I don't want to keep you, but thanks again for the pickles," Michael said, raising a hand in farewell and turning to go.

"Anytime. I will definitely barter for bread." Eu laughed.

"Perfect!" Michael laughed, too, and it was music to Eu's ears.

While the chicken was cooking, she whipped up a savory coleslaw and put forkfuls of bread-and-butter pickles into a small bowl to enjoy with her dinner. Feeling proud of herself for making a tasty and healthy meal, she opened a bottle of wine and softened a stick of butter in the microwave to spread on the amazing bread Michael had brought.

Eu scrolled through email on her phone as she savored the delicious food, and much to her delight, she saw one of the writing jobs she'd applied for had offered her an ongoing gig. Munching on a crunchy crust of bread, she tapped out an acceptance, planning to get started on the first assignment right after dinner.

When the dinner dishes were washed, and the leftovers were placed in containers and arranged in the fridge, Eu made herself a cup of herbal tea and set up her phone to use as a hotspot with her laptop so that she could access the internet without having a service run to the cabin.

She'd just gotten into the depths of typing a comprehensive outline for her first article when yet another loud knock on the door nearly made her jump out of her skin. The sky had gone dark, and she glanced at her phone to see the time, which apparently had flown while she was writing.

Uncertain as to whether or not it would be wise to open her door at this hour, she was weighing the pros and cons of it when the pounding sounded again. It had to be the obnoxious realtor, and this time, Eu decided, she was going to give the brash woman a piece of her mind. She also made a mental note to have a peephole installed sooner rather than later.

Frustrated, she marched to the door, flipping lights on throughout the cabin as she went, and yanked it open with a frown on her face. She nearly gasped in surprise when she saw two grim-faced uniformed deputies on her porch. One was tall and had a shadow of dark stubble along his jaw. His nameplate identified him as Carter. The other deputy, Writman, was shorter, but thickly muscled, his hair in a short crew cut.

"Oh! Hello," she greeted them.

"Eugenia Barkley?" Carter asked, his southern accent profound.

"Yes?" Eu replied, frowning. "Is something wrong?"

"I'm Deputy Carter, and this is Deputy Writman. May we come in?"

"Uh, sure. What's this about?" Eu asked, letting them file into the cabin.

"Ma'am, are you familiar with a Sue-Lynn Matlock?" Writman asked.

Eu took a breath and folded her arms, trying to slow the spike of adrenaline that always seemed to course through her around authority figures like policemen and bosses.

"She's a realtor here in Summerset Beach," Carter added.

"Right, the realtor," Eu blurted, nodding. "Yeah, actually, I just met her today. Somehow, I don't think she's going to be on my favorite person list."

Carter and Writman exchanged a glance.

"Oh?" Writman said. "And why is that?"

"Because she came over this morning to ask me about listing this cabin for sale and I told her I'd contact her when I was ready to list it. Then, later in the day, I found her standing out on my back deck. She'd found a key under a rock or something and had just decided to let herself in. Nearly scared me to death. So, she tried to badger me about listing, and I told her to leave. Can you imagine the nerve of someone just letting themselves in like that?"

"Is it true that you made pickles recently?" Carter asked.

"Yes, I did. Oh, my gosh, can you still smell them? I guess I'm immune to the aroma since I live here, but I don't mind vinegar anyway." Eu shrugged.

"Did you give Ms. Matlock any of your pickles?" Writman asked.

"No, definitely not. When I saw her standing out there and she told me how she'd gotten in, the only thing on my mind was making her leave."

Carter dug down into his pocket and produced a plastic bag with a piece of paper in it. He held it out for Eu to see. "Is this your handwriting?" he asked.

It was the note from Crappie Callie that had been left with the returned jars of pickles.

"No, but...where did you get that? Did you pick it up as you were coming in? I forgot to bring those jars of pickles in from the front porch."

"It was at Sue-Lynn's house," Writman replied.

"Well, how on earth could that have happened?" Eu wondered aloud. Then, realization struck. "I forgot to bring those pickles in. I bet the note stuck to one of the jars and the realtor must have stolen them when she left," she exclaimed, shaking her head. "What a piece of work."

"Well, that would be convenient, now wouldn't it?" Carter said. "We're going to need you to provide a writing sample."

"I'd be happy to. But why in the world would you need one from me?" Eu asked.

"Because Sue-Lynn Matlock was found dead in her kitchen, with a half-eaten jar of pickles on the table, and this note on the floor next to her," Carter replied, tucking the note back into his pocket. "Looks like foul play, and you've officially become a person of interest in the case. Now, let's have that writing sample."

"Dead? Wow, that's intense. But you can't be serious about me being a person of interest in the case. I just got here, for crying out loud. Besides, I don't kill people. I'm from Los Angeles."

"Yeah, there's no way an outsider would kill someone. They'd be plumb crazy to do that, huh?" Writman said dryly.

"Ma'am, it'd be best all the way around if you'd just give us a writing sample right now," Carter directed.

"Fine. Do you literally want me to just sit down and write something?"

"We weren't born yesterday, city girl. How about you find something you wrote in the past, so you can't pretend to write differently now that you've seen the note?" Writman drawled.

"City girl? Wow, that's professional," Eu snapped. "Would you like my grocery list from today? It's in my purse."

"That'll do," Carter replied.

Eu tried to keep her hands from shaking with anger, fear, and adrenaline as she dug in her purse for the list. When she found it, she handed it over to Carter.

"There. Happy?" she asked.

"We'll be taking this with us. Don't leave town," Carter replied.

"Like I have somewhere else to go," Eu muttered under her breath, feeling tears prick her eyelids as she followed them to the door.

CHAPTER NINE

Concentrating hard enough to finish the outline for her article was an impossible task, so Eu had a glass of wine while brooding on the deck, then headed inside for a hot bath and bed.

Sleep didn't come easily, and when she'd stared at the ceiling after waking up for what had to be at least the hundredth time, Eu grabbed her phone to check the time and saw that it was 4:37 a.m. "Well, Dad and I used to go fishing at this hour, so there's no reason to lay here being miserable. Maybe some fresh air will help me clear my head."

She made a thermos of coffee after dressing quickly and used her cell phone as a flashlight when she headed down to the fishing hole, which, as promised, was well lit, shining like a beacon of hope in the darkness of a Missouri morning.

Crappie Callie was in her usual spot, slumped in her chair, staring at the tip of her pole, when Eu entered the shack around the fishing hole and this time, she didn't even bother to glance up. Eu unfolded her chair and plopped down in her seat across from the old prune, without so much as a word. Every other time she'd greeted her, it had been pointless, so why bother now?

When she lifted the lid of her Styrofoam bait bucket, her minnows weren't swimming very vigorously, but she dipped her hand in and grabbed one anyway. The flopping little fish had barely disappeared beneath the surface and Eu's pole nearly bent in half with the force of a giant bite.

Reeling steadily, as whatever was on the end of her line fought a valiant battle, Eu realized she still didn't have a net to scoop her catch into so she could lift it out of the water. Michael's net was on the wall behind her, and she turned to glance at it longingly.

"I can do this," she muttered, thinking.

She stopped reeling when she saw the first flashes of bright green scales below the surface, and slowly backed toward the net, letting out a bit of line to keep the fish under the water. Holding her pole with one hand, she reached for the net with the other and tucked it under her arm so she could reel in the line she'd let out. When Eu moved forward and reached the rail at the edge of the fishing hole, she held her pole in one hand and used the net to scoop the fish out, breathing a sigh of relief when she finally lowered the net, with its flopping captive, carefully to the deck.

She'd landed a massive crappie, much to her delight, but when she realized she had no one to celebrate with, her enthusiasm ebbed a bit. She slipped it into the basket she'd bought from Trixie and lowered it back into the water.

She baited up and dropped her line into the water again, then poured herself a cup of coffee from the thermos she'd brought. Right after she took her first sip, Callie got a bite and reeled in a much smaller crappie than Eu had, which gave Eu no small measure of petty satisfaction as she enjoyed her coffee.

Callie's pole bounced with another giant bite as soon as she dropped her line back into the water. Eu watched the older woman wrestle with what looked like a whale on the end of her line, but her inner sportswoman had to do the right thing.

"Do you want some help?" she asked, setting her coffee down.

Callie didn't even dignify her question with a grunt, so Eu folded her arms and watched the spectacle. Callie rose from her chair, reeling with great effort.

Eu's pole then bounced so hard it nearly flew from her hand, and she started reeling.

"Oh, this is a big one," she bellowed, her biceps and forearms straining with effort.

Glad that she'd left Michael's net leaning up against the railing, Eu struggled and fought until she saw a huge bass break the surface. Grabbing the net, she scooped it up and brought it in. Thrilled beyond measure, she deposited it in the basket with the crappie and noticed that Callie was still fighting her fish.

"Oh, for crying out loud, quit being too stubborn to ask for help," she muttered, trudging over to Callie's side of the fishing hole and slipping the net under a fish that made her bass look like a goldfish.

It was the biggest catfish she'd ever seen in real life, and after using both hands and every ounce of her strength to lift it up and over the rail, Eu marveled at the sheer size of it.

"Wow, that's amazing!" she exclaimed as the catfish let out fierce gawping sounds of protest.

Callie ignored her completely and stepped around Eu to take the catfish off of her line. She dropped the beast into her basket, lowered it into the water, and opened her bait bucket, without a word.

Eu stared at her, open-mouthed, then picked up the net.

"You're welcome," she muttered.

She hung Michael's net back up on the wall, gathered her things, and stomped toward the exit. On her way back up the hill, she passed Michael.

"You're up early," he commented, his warm smile nearly bringing tears to her eyes.

"Couldn't sleep," she replied with a shrug.

"Even with all this fresh air? That's too bad," he commented, peering at her in the faint first light of morning. "You okay?"

"Yeah, I will be. I'm just feeling like it was probably a big mistake to even come here in the first place. But I'll be fine. I always am…somehow." Eu sighed, too weary and frustrated to pretend.

"Anything I can do?"

Eu shook her head. "No, but thanks for asking."

"No problem. Let me know if I can help. I mean it."

"I will. Thanks."

Eu tried to smile and continued on to the cabin. She had fish to clean, and after that, she planned on eating as much of the massive bass as she possibly could for breakfast.

While she was frying the bass, keeping the deck doors open and the ceiling fans running to vent the aroma to the outdoors, Eu's phone rang. Her heart leapt with joy when she saw Fran's photo pop up on her phone.

"Hey, you," she said, holding the phone to her ear with her shoulder while sliding a spatula carefully under the huge bass filet.

Fran wasted no time in getting to the point.

"Eu, what the heck have you gotten yourself into out there? I had a sheriff's deputy contact me asking a bunch of questions about you and pickles or something. Are you out in the middle of nowhere? The deputy who called sounded so much like Deputy Dawg that I thought I was being punked."

Bad situation or not, that made Eu smile. She explained what had happened when the deputies showed up at her door, and by the time she was finished, she was able to plate her perfectly cooked bass and take it to the table so she could eat while she talked. The outside of the filets were golden brown and crispy, and the meat was tender and tasty.

"Holy cow, Eu? Murder? What kind of a place are you in? That does it. I'm coming out there. I'm not going to leave you alone if there's a murderer around. We can take shifts sleeping or whatever," Fran insisted.

"No, don't do that. I'm fine. Murderers are usually related to their victims in some way, like family, coworkers, acquaintances, or whatever. I'm sure whoever killed the realtor doesn't even know I exist," Eu replied, shaking a bit of salt onto the bass.

There was a moment of silence.

"The degree of what you retain from all those true crime TV shows you watch is a little disturbing. I hear what you're saying, but I'm coming out there anyway. When I go in to work today, I'll talk to Jett about filling in for me at the shop while I'm gone."

"I'll teach you how to fish." Eu chuckled.

"Don't threaten me young lady. Gross," Fran replied. Eu could picture the exact way she was undoubtedly wrinkling her nose.

They chatted for a few more minutes and hung up. Eu stashed the uneaten portion of her fish in a container in the fridge and looked on her phone for an internet provider. Since she was going to have to stick around for a while, she might as well get service started. After calling the only provider in the area and being told the soonest she'd be able to get hooked up would be in four-six weeks, Eu hung up, frustrated, and grabbed her laptop anyway. She might not have internet service at the cabin, but she could at least get online by making her phone a hotspot.

"Investigate first, write my articles later," she muttered, logging on. The call from Fran, just hearing her bestie's voice, warmed her heart and inspired her to get proactive.

CHAPTER TEN

"Okay, Sue-Lynn Matlock, let's see who you are and why someone would want to kill you," Eu said, her eyes scanning the screen as she typed search terms into her browser.

She discovered the basics. Sue-Lynn was divorced, owned her own home, didn't have any kids, and was very successful.

"Oh, wait, what do we have here?" Eu said, finding an article about an award the realtor had won. It had been awarded the night she'd been discovered dead. There was another realtor standing next to her in the photo that went with the article, who looked less than happy.

"Who is that?" Eu wondered aloud. "Paula Pinson, runner-up. Ohhhh…no wonder she doesn't look happy. Well, Paula Pinson, I'll be looking up info on you too, because you just became a suspect."

Just after Eu typed in Paula Pinson's name, there was a knock on the door. After the past couple days, that simple sound made her heart race.

"Please don't be those obnoxious deputies," she muttered, heading to the door.

The perfectly put-together man in a suit, who clearly had used product in his hair, made Eu supremely aware of her less than stellar appearance and the lingering scent of fried fish in the air. He was good looking but seemed very out of place in Summerset Beach. Like a stockbroker who'd wandered into the wilderness.

"Hi, there," he greeted her with a hundred-watt smile. "Sorry to just drop in on you. My name is Kyle Bresden." He handed Eu a business card and she noted he was a developer before putting it in her pocket.

"Hi, I'm Eu."

The man's smile didn't falter, but he stared at her. "Uh… I'm sorry, you said your name was?"

"Oh, right. It's Eugenia," she replied.

"Well, that's beautiful. A family name?"

"No. My mom just chose to inflict it upon me. Is there something I can help you with?" Eu asked, itching to get back to her online sleuthing.

"I was just admiring your cabin and wondering what your plans were for it." Kyle gave her a disarming smile and shrugged.

"I guess I'm still trying to figure that out."

"You literally have the best spot on this entire peninsula. This place could easily be worth millions if you tore down the cabin and built a more luxurious home here. Do you mind if I come in and take a look around? See the views and such?" he asked.

"I'm sorry, but I'm right in the middle of a project for work," Eu replied, miffed by the suggestion that the cabin should be torn down.

"Oh, okay. What are you working on?" he asked, apparently not catching her not-so-subtle hint that she had things to do.

"I can't really talk about it. I'm a reporter."

"In the middle of the woods in Missouri?"

Eu simply stared at him.

"None of my business. Got it," he said, holding up his hands in mock surrender. "I'll let you get back to it. If you ever decide you want to bulldoze this place and start over, let me know." He flashed her a quick smile and slipped into the driver's seat of a sports car that looked as out of place as he did.

Stunned, Eu stared after the car as it pulled away, then shut the door and leaned against it, tears springing to her eyes. She may not have known her mother, but the cabin was all she had left of her. Wondering about her reaction, she shook her head and took some deep breaths in an attempt to regain her composure. "Guess we never know what we've got until someone offers to bulldoze it," she said softly.

Still rattled from the encounter and the feelings that rose up within her as a result of it, Eu decided to take a break. A walk to the general store to get fresh minnows might help her clear her head.

"Hi, Trixie," Eu greeted the proprietor, who was doing a word search puzzle behind the counter and taking occasional bites from a piece of beef jerky.

"Saw Bresden parked at your cabin." Trixie made it sound like an accusation. "Sure hope you didn't sell out to that snake."

"Huh?" Eu said, setting her minnow bucket down by the giant aquarium. "What do you mean?"

Trixie came around the corner and reached for the minnow net, regarding Eu with what looked like suspicion.

"That lowdown, money-grubbing hustler has been pestering every owner in this complex to sell out. He only needs one more to agree and he'll have enough to kick the rest out. If you sell your property to him, every other owner in here may lose everything they've ever invested in this place," Trixie said, scooping up minnows and depositing them into Eu's bucket as she spoke.

Eu gasped. "That's awful. How is that even possible?" she asked.

"Dumb covenants. Apparently, the original developer wasn't very detail oriented. Instead of requiring unanimous support, or even a majority, it only takes a handful of folks to cave and the rest of us are up the crick without a paddle."

"Well, I definitely won't be selling my cabin to him, then. If I decide to sell, it'll be to another person who wants it for their own use," Eu replied.

Trixie turned, her net hovering over the water, and stared at Eu. "It ain't about just you. What if you sell to someone and they sell out? The rest of us will still lose everything. I'm just gonna tell you straight up, there's a lot resting on your shoulders. Maybe if your mama gave you this place, she did it for a reason. Maybe you should think about that."

Trixie added a few more minnows to the bucket and headed for the register. Eu paid, thanked her, and left, feeling the older woman's eyes drilling through her as she exited.

"Why did my mother leave this place to me?" she wondered, taking in the incredible beauty around her. "That woman never even sent me a birthday or Christmas card."

The thought stayed with her as she chopped and diced and seasoned and spiced a large pot of homemade fish chowder. She decided that once she'd had a nice healthy bowl of the hearty chowder that she was preparing from memory, she'd snoop around the cabin a bit more and try to find an answer as to why it had been gifted to her in the first place. The chowder was a dish that she knew and loved, and right about now, she could use the familiar comfort of the hearty soup.

Just when she tasted the chowder for the last time before loading up a bowl with it, there was a knock at her door.

"Seriously? What now?" she muttered, turning the chowder down to the lowest setting and covering the pot.

When she went to the door this time, however, she was glad to see a friendly face.

"Wow, whatever you're cooking in there smells delicious," Michael commented. "I just dropped by to see if you were okay."

"Yeah, I'm fine, and thanks. I just finished a big batch of fish chowder if you want to come in and have some lunch," Eu offered, astonished by her own boldness. But then again, she did kind of owe him some gratitude for being the only person who had been consistently nice to her since she arrived in Summerset Beach.

"I'd love to, thanks."

"Great. Come on in. I have some of your homemade bread left that we can eat with the chowder. It'll be perfect."

"Sounds great," Michael agreed, following her inside. "I think we should eat out on the deck so we're visible to the neighbors. People just love any excuse to spread wild rumors around here," he said.

Eu shook her head. "That's ridiculous. I sometimes wonder what I've gotten myself into, coming out here."

"Well, it's definitely not Los Angeles," Michael replied.

"Not even close. It's so beautiful though," Eu mused, glancing out the massive dining room windows. "Why don't you go ahead and get settled on the deck, and I'll bring everything out."

"Will do. I'll be enjoying the best view in Summerset Beach."

Eu sliced the still delicious bread on a cutting board and took it out to the deck table with a container of butter, then came back into the house for the chowder. Setting the bowls on the table, she said, "I have sparkling water, iced tea, or milk."

"Iced tea, please," Michael replied, placing the cloth napkin she'd handed him in his lap.

They ate in silence for a while and Eu was secretly relieved. She had outdone herself with the chowder. The fresh fish had made all the difference in the world.

"This is beyond delicious," Michael said, dipping a crust of bread into his bowl.

"Thanks. I'm glad you like it."

"I'm sorry you've had such a hard time since you've been here," Michael said after swallowing.

"I've wondered so many times if I've lost my mind even thinking this would work out somehow. I can't imagine why my mother left me this place. Did you know her?" Eu asked.

"Just enough to say hi and bye, you know, a neighborly kind of thing. She was beautiful, a clone of you, but more... I don't know, high maintenance? Heckuva fisherman though."

Eu's eyebrow rose, and her spoon stopped halfway to her mouth. "I always thought she was just a spoiled rich girl."

"I try to keep in mind that most people are far more complex than what anyone sees on the outside. And then there's the fact that you've only heard about her from one source. From what I understood, she came here to get away from her life. She was always alone and was very down to earth and nice to everyone."

"Now I don't know what to think…" Eu mused, scooping a good sized chunk of potato out of her chowder with her spoon.

"I've found that some of my best discoveries are made when all my assumptions have been blown out of the water. So, I saw that Kyle Bresden came by," Michael said, changing the subject, for which Eu was entirely grateful. "How did that go?"

"He seemed nice enough at first, I guess, but the more he talked, the more he seemed like he was… I don't know, a little too slick or something. Anyway, I didn't let him get past the doorstep, and as he was leaving, he said something about bulldozing this cabin, which really ticked me off."

"Understandably." Michael nodded.

"Then I went up to the general store to get some minnows and Trixie told me about how ridiculous the original covenants are, which puts a whole lot of pressure on my decision-making. Yeah, it's been a banner day. Thanks for letting me vent, I hope I didn't ruin your meal."

Michael smiled. "Not at all. This chowder way too good for that. But yeah, the original charter for this complex was designed with tourism in mind, not residency. Residents spend enough money here to get by with their daily needs met, mostly. Tourists throw their money around like they have printing presses in their basement."

"Seems like life always comes down to money, doesn't it?" Eu sighed. "And I have none, so I guess I just don't count."

"There's more to life than money, Eu. Some of us have a world of riches and we don't even realize it," Michael replied gently, standing and picking up his dishes. "Thank you for lunch. I truly enjoyed both the food and the company," he said, heading for the kitchen.

"You're welcome. Thanks for being easy to talk to."

"Anytime. Can I help you with the dishes?" he asked.

"No, I'll take care of those. Can't have the neighbors thinking things." Eu rolled her eyes and Michael chuckled.

"Good point. Enjoy the rest of your day," he said, setting his dishes down next to the sink and heading for the door.

"You too," Eu called out, already missing the presence of another human.

After finishing the dishes, she wiped her waterlogged hands on a towel and glanced around the cabin. "Okay, it's time to go hunting for clues about the mysterious Miranda Bellingham."

CHAPTER ELEVEN

Eu didn't know where to start looking for clues about her mother, so she wandered around inside the cabin, trying to form a picture of the mysterious woman who came to such a humble place to get away from her world of wealth and glamour.

She noted the color schemes of the rooms in the cabin were clearly based upon the soft blues and greens that could easily be seen just by looking out of the nearest window.

"I wonder if these were her favorite colors," she murmured to herself, running the heavy blue silk of the bedroom drapes through her fingers.

"She came here alone, and she actually fished," Eu mused, gazing out at the water. "That's not even remotely consistent with what I've been told about her."

Wandering from room to room, searching in closets and under beds, Eu realized something. There was absolutely nothing personal about the décor or contents of the house. There were no photos or address books, or even purses or clothing.

In the living room, Eu glanced at an amazing painting that somehow managed to perfectly capture the view of the sunset from the cabin's deck. When she looked more closely at the painting, she saw the initials MB on it.

"My mother was a painter?" Her brows rose. "There were definitely some things that Dad either didn't know or forgot to tell me about." The thought weighed heavily on her. Had she been resenting someone for all these years who maybe didn't deserve her scorn?

Eu shook herself. "Wandering around trying to figure out who my mother was isn't getting me any closer to catching a killer and clearing my name," she muttered. "I need to go find out more about Sue-

Lynn. There has to be a reason someone decided to do such a heinous thing."

Tucking the emotions regarding her mother back into the closed-off part of her heart where she'd hidden them for her entire life, Eu took a breath, squared her shoulders, and grabbed her purse, heading out to do something constructive.

"Wow," she breathed, after parking the scooter Trixie had rented to her a few blocks away and walking up to Sue-Lynn's house on foot. The place was huge and very well kept.

"I hope she doesn't have security cameras," Eu muttered, walking around the outside of the house.

She hurried away from the street side of the house where she might be seen and took her time examining her surroundings on the side of the house with a tall hedge that would hopefully give her some cover.

Eu crept over to the house and stood on her tiptoes to peer into a window. The interior was dark, and the only thing she could see, even when she cupped her hands around her eyes, were the shadowy outlines of what looked like massive furniture.

"Hey! What do you think you're doing over there!" a gruff male voice demanded, making Eu jump back from the window, her cheeks reddening. A man in jeans and a western shirt, who looked like a sad counterfeit of the Marlboro Man, busy mustache and all, stared at her, hands on his hips.

"Uh… hi." Eu's mind raced for a plausible explanation. She finally settled on something close to the truth. "I'm ummm… that is, I'm looking for my realtor. I've been calling and calling, and she hasn't responded, so I'm trying to see if she's here."

"Well, I hate to disappoint ya, hon, but you ain't gonna find her here. Somebody killed her and if you've been working with her for any length of time, that probably don't surprise you none."

"Oh, how awful," Eu breathed, going intentionally wide-eyed. "Poor Sue-Lynn. Are you a client of hers too?"

"Heck no. I'm smart enough not to do business with that woman, no offense. I dated her for a few years, 'til I couldn't take it no more." He shrugged.

The ex-boyfriend!

"Oh, well, uh… I'm so sorry for your loss. I'm Kate. Kate Hepburn." Eu stuck out her hand, hoping he wasn't an old film buff. He shook it, lingering just a bit too long.

"Nice to meetcha, Miss Kate. I'm Beau, Beau Garet. You single, Miss Kate?" he asked, appraising Eu from head to toe. She suddenly was more than aware she was in a location that couldn't be seen from the road.

"No, I'm not. I'm engaged." Eu smiled, pretending she wasn't uncomfortable at all.

Beau's eyes flicked down to her left hand, where no ring supported her declaration.

"You ain't from around here, are ya?" His eyes narrowed as he peered closely at her.

"No, I'm not. Sue-Lynn was showing me resort properties. Are you here to take care of her plants or something?" she asked, injecting as much innocent curiosity as she could into her voice.

"I'm thinking it ain't none of your business why I'm here, lady," Beau said, taking a step toward her.

"You're right, it isn't. I was just trying to have a conversation, my bad. Anyway, nice meeting you,

Beau," she said, hurrying past and preparing to defend herself if necessary.

He let her pass, and once she was out of sight around the corner of the house, Eu broke into a dead run. She darted to her scooter, plunked her helmet down on her head, turned the engine over, and tore out of Sue-Lynn's neighborhood as fast as she could.

Taking deep breaths in through her nose to slow her breathing and rapid heart rate, Eu was relieved that, even if she had nearly been attacked, she now had information she didn't have before. Sue-Lynn had an ex-boyfriend who wasn't very happy with her. He also seemed to have a bit of a temper problem.

She may have just had a face-to-face interaction with an actual killer.

The thought made her blood run cold, but it also made her more determined to figure out who had killed Sue-Lynn. It was time to go home and do some digging on the internet.

CHAPTER TWELVE

Eu drank two glasses of water and fixed herself a snack before curling up on the couch and tapping Beau Garet's name into her phone.

"Okay, Mr. Creepy Ex-Boyfriend, let's see what we can find out about you," she mused, scrolling through the results. She stopped and frowned down at her phone. "Oh, wow, that guy actually owns and operates a booze cruise boat?" She read further, then scrolled down to another article.

"Whoa... he had an argument with Sue-Lynn at a country club dinner. She shoved him into the buffet, and he was thrown out. Well, isn't that classy? But being publicly embarrassed could be a good motive for murder."

Eu opened another tab and dug a bit deeper into Beau Garet's life. His business was mentioned in an article from the local newspaper last year as one that had been hit hard by a slowdown in tourism.

"He's struggling with his business, and she's successful. More motive."

Some old posts on one of Sue-Lynn's social media sites included photos and captions that showed she'd bought Beau the boat he used for his booze cruises.

"Yikes, she was his sugar mama," Eu said, scrolling through several images that had recorded the celebration of Beau opening his company, with Sue-Lynn at his side, bankrolling the whole thing.

Feeling certain that she may have just positively identified the realtor's killer, Eu decided to cover her bases by finishing the research she'd started into Sue-Lynn's real estate rival, Paula Pinson.

The first thing that popped up, of course, was Paula, standing proudly with a real estate sign that had her phone number and office location on it.

"Well, then, Paula Pinson, if you're going to make it that easy, I guess I'll put my reporter hat on and pay you an investigative visit."

Before she could change her mind, she grabbed her keys and helmet and headed out the door.

A darkly tanned receptionist beamed at her when she entered the real estate office. "Hi, there! How may I help you?" she asked, her southern accent thick, but charming.

"Hi. I saw Paula Pinson on a billboard, and I wondered if she's taking new clients," Eu replied. It was true, she had seen the realtor's face on a billboard on her way over.

"She sure is," the receptionist announced brightly. "Let me just call back to her. You can have a seat, and she'll come get you."

"Great, thanks," Eu replied. She sat down on a chenille sofa that had a snag on one of the arms and didn't have to wait long. Paula Pinson came out to greet her, a bit shorter and thicker than the billboards had indicated, but with the same genial smile. She didn't look like a killer, but then, most killers were very good at fooling people from what Eu had seen on documentaries.

"Well, hello! I'm Paula," the realtor trilled, approaching Eu and sticking out her hand.

Eu shook it. "Hi, I'm Eugenia," she replied, wincing inwardly when she realized she should have used a different name.

Paula led her back to an office where sales trophies and photos with what looked like local dignitaries lined the walls. Her desk was heavy and baroque, but the room, aside from the display of accolades, was tastefully decorated.

"Have a seat, hon," she waved a hand casually at one of the paisley club chairs in front of the desk. Eu sat. "Now, how can I help you?" she asked.

"Well, I'm new in town, and… this is kind of awkward, but my realtor uh… passed recently, and now I need someone to list my house when I'm ready," Eu said.

"Oh, darlin', I'm so sorry! Wait… were you working with Sue-Lynn?" Paula asked, her smile fading.

"Yes, I was. We didn't exactly hit it off right away, but I didn't know who else to go to, so I stuck with her," Eu replied, hoping to draw a reaction from Paula.

The realtor shook her head. "You poor thing. I hate that you came to our beautiful area and got hooked up with someone like her."

"Really? Why? Was she not a good realtor or something?" Eu asked, feigning innocence.

"Oh, no, she was a great realtor, if you think someone being so ruthless that she doesn't have any friends fits that description." Paula made a face.

"I wondered about that. She seemed to have an edge to her, and then someone killed her." Eu faked a shudder. "I mean, I don't like to victim blame, but there must've been some reason, right?"

Paula nodded. "Girl, I'm not gonna judge you. I thought the very same thing. Sue-Lynn would stop at nothing to get what she wanted, and I was thinking that she may have gone too far."

"I mean, I get that, but I just can't imagine who on earth would do such a thing. Everyone I've met here is just so nice," Eu replied.

"Overall, yep, we're a friendly community, but between you and me..." Paula leaned over the desk and lowered her voice. "They say that usually, these kinds of things are personal. I really feel like it was either her ex-boyfriend or another realtor in her office who did the deed. She swindled that poor woman out of what would have been a multi-million-dollar deal."

"Oh, wow. Yeah, money can be a powerful motivator, I guess."

"For folks who are inclined to walk that line, I suppose so." Paula shrugged and shook her head. "Now, enough about all that. What can I do for you, Eugenia? You need to buy a house? Sell one? What can I show you?"

"I think for now, I'd just like to see what's going on in this market so that I can decide what I'd like to do. Is there any way you could run an analysis for me?" Eu asked.

Paula's face fell. "Well, I'm sorry if my candor offended you in some way," she snipped, shuffling some papers on her desk.

"Oh, no, not at all," Eu assured her. "I'll just need some information before I make any decisions."

"Understand. I'll see what I can do," she said, her tone having cooled significantly.

Eu's stomach growled as she headed toward home, so she stopped at a BBQ joint at the water's edge that clearly catered to tourists. On the street in front of the restaurant, a small hand painted sign with the name of Beau's booze cruise business on it featured an arrow pointing to the right.

More convinced than ever that Beau was Sue-Lynn's killer, she hoped that maybe she could get some info from someone local about him.

The smell of mouth-watering barbeque enveloped her when she opened the door to the restaurant. The hostess led her to a table by the window so that she could look out over the water. As one of only a handful of patrons, Eu hoped she might be able to get some decent information from her server, a tired-looking woman about her age.

"There ya go, ma'am," the server said, placing a heaping plate of barbequed brisket and all the fixings, including a fluffy golden-brown biscuit, in front of her. "Can I get you anything else?"

"This looks delicious, thank you. I have a quick question if you don't mind," Eu replied.

"Sure, no problem. It ain't like I'm overrun with customers right now." The server smiled.

"Great, thanks. I'm not from here, and I'm looking for things to do. What do you think about the boat tour? I saw the sign in front of this building."

"Honestly, I'm not really a fan. You'd do better to rent a boat yourself and go exploring. But if you decide to go, stay away from the owner. He's always on board and tries to pick up the pretty women. Also has a wicked temper. The whole town knows about it."

"I'll keep it in mind. Kinda weird though, you'd think that someone who owned a business like that would have a wife or a girlfriend or something."

"Just between you, me, and the fence post…" the server glanced about and lowered her voice. "That sorry excuse for a man had lots of girlfriends even when he had someone at home waiting for him."

"Order up!" a voice barked from behind the server, making her jump.

"I gotta run, but you just holler if you need anything, okay?" she said, dashing away.

"Oh, I think I got everything I need," Eu whispered, turning her attention toward the plate of joy in front of her.

After she ate until she could eat no more, Eu boxed up her leftovers and headed for home with them safely tucked in one of the scooter's saddlebags.

Her porch and deck lights weren't on since she'd left the cabin well before dark. Creeped out after stories of murder and perhaps coming face-to-face with the man who had done the deed, Eu used her phone to find her way to the door and unlock it.

With her bag of leftovers in one hand, she flipped on the foyer light switch with the other, and nothing happened. Her heart thumping in her chest, she tried each of the three other switches, with the same result. Locking the door and pulling it shut behind her as she backed out of the house, Eu did the only thing she could think of. She jogged to Michael's cabin, her phone lighting the way, his porch light a beacon in the darkness.

Keeping an eye on the route between her house and his, she rapped on the door. Nothing. She rapped again, harder this time. Still nothing.

"He's gotta be at the fishing hole," she murmured, scared and frustrated.

"Hey, neighbor," he greeted her.

"I'm so glad I found you here." Eu blew out a breath, relieved.

"I am too. Anything wrong?"

"The power is out at my cabin."

"That's strange, mine was on when I left," he mused.

"It's on now, too, but mine isn't," Eu explained.

"Well then, let me reel this in and we'll go have a look."

They headed up to the cabin, this time with Michael using his cell phone to locate and open her fuse box.

"There's the problem," he said, frowning.

"What? What's the problem?" Eu asked, unnerved by his sudden change in demeanor. It had to be something bad to cause the perpetually laid-back professor to actually frown.

"The main line to your cabin has been cut. This isn't wear and tear or an accident, it was intentional.

Someone had to shut the breakers down to make it happen or they would've been fried," Michael said, staring at the wires under the box.

"Intentional?" Eu swallowed hard.

"Yeah. I think you should come to my cabin and call the police. You can stay there, safe and sound, until they arrive."

Eu nodded and followed Michael to his cabin, trying hard not to notice that he'd picked up his pace and kept glancing over his shoulder as they walked.

CHAPTER THIRTEEN

Thankfully, the deputies who came to check out Eu's cabin weren't the same ones who had accused her of being involved in Sue-Lynn's murder. The two very professional deputies asked Eu what had happened, then requested she stay at Michael's cabin until they were able to determine whether or not there was an intruder still inside her house.

They returned a few minutes later, confirming Michael's assessment that the lines had indeed been cut, and told Eu it was safe to go back to the cabin.

"Want me to walk with you?" Michael asked after the deputies left.

"Yeah, that would be great. Thank you," Eu said, her heart filling with dread.

"I can go in with you while you check things out if you'd like," he offered.

"I think I'll be okay. The deputies said there was no one inside," Eu said, taking a deep breath.

"You sure?" Michael asked gently.

"Yeah, I'm good." Eu nodded.

"I'm just down the road if you need anything. Try to get some sleep," Michael replied, turning to go.

"I will. Thanks again," Eu said, hating to see him go, but knowing it would be unfair to impose on him further. He'd already been a huge help.

The house was quiet and would be pitch dark until morning, so she used her phone to navigate to the kitchen where there was a drawer with matches and candles. Eu lit a candle and used it to light a large jar candle in her room, as well as a smaller jar candle in the bathroom. Her hair brush was on the counter in the bathroom, which was puzzling. She could have sworn she'd left it on the vanity in her bedroom.

Had someone moved it, or was she just being paranoid? Her pulse thrummed with momentary fear and goosebumps rose on her upper arms.

It didn't matter. At the moment, she needed to contact the power company emergency line. Sitting in the glow of a vanilla cookie scented jar candle, Eu made the call and was informed they'd send out a team in the morning, but if there had been damage to the line, she'd be charged for the repairs. Too exhausted to argue, she hung up and gathered her toothbrush, which was about four inches from where she remembered setting it that morning, to go brush her teeth before bed.

When she looked at her phone in the glow of the candlelight, Eu noted with dismay that her battery was dangerously low, and without power, she couldn't even charge it.

"Oh, wait," she said, remembering. "There are electrical outlets in the fishing hole. I can go fishing in the morning and charge my phone."

Satisfied she was relatively safe; Eu checked all the doors and windows one last time before slipping under the covers. Sleep didn't come easily, and when she did drift off, she had a series of small nightmares that woke her up time and again.

Eu's eyes felt grainy behind her eyelids when she finally opened them and decided to get up, though she felt far from rested. There was enough battery left in her phone to let her know that the sun wouldn't be up for more than an hour, but she intended to go to the fishing hole anyway. She needed to charge her phone, and it was pointless to stay in a cabin where she couldn't even make coffee. Besides, the fishing hole felt somehow… safe, familiar. After last night's electrical incident, she hated to admit that her cozy cabin didn't feel as safe as the fishing hole, no matter how irrational that might seem.

There was a bit of a bite in the air when she went down to the fishing hole, and Eu was glad that she'd put on a hoodie with her cargo shorts and tank top.

"Morning!" Michael greeted her. "Thought you might need coffee this morning, so I brought you some, and some strawberry strudel too, if you're hungry. It's over on the shelf whenever you're done getting set up."

"You're the best," Eu groaned, grateful. "But how on earth do you stay in such good shape when you're that good at baking?"

"I swim laps every morning." Michael shrugged. "The pool is heated, so even on mornings like this, I can get my laps in."

"On mornings like this I do well to even get out of bed," Eu grumbled, wandering over to fix herself some coffee even before getting her line in the water.

"How are you holding up?" Michael asked, looking concerned.

"Things could definitely be better. I had a run in yesterday with Sue-Lynn's ex-boyfriend that was less than pleasant," Eu replied.

"I've heard he has a temper."

"You can say that again. It wouldn't surprise me at all if he was the one who cut my power lines."

Michael drew in a breath and shook his head. "Yeah, you might want to be extra aware of your surroundings for a little while."

"So much for small towns being safer than cities. I never encountered anything like this in LA. This strudel is amazing by the way."

"Thanks, it's my own recipe."

Before Eu could reply, her phone rang. "That was the power company," she told Michael after hanging up. "They're on their way."

"Good. If you want to leave your phone here, I'll keep an eye on it while you're gone."

"Thanks. I'll be back once they're here and doing their thing," Eu promised, heading up the trail just as the sun began to peek over the horizon.

She paced in front of her cabin for ten minutes before the power company techs arrived, and once they saw the problem and went to work on fixing it, she headed back down to the fishing hole.

"They're taking care of it," she announced.

"Great," Michael said, his hand poised over his pole as he watched it intently. Eu knew without asking that he must've had a good bite. He pulled in a respectable crappie and put it in his basket. "Your phone was really blowing up while you were gone. I didn't look at it, but the notifications just kept coming in," he told Eu as he was re-baiting his hook.

"Three calls from Paula Pinson. Wow, is the real estate biz really that competitive around here?" she said, gazing at her phone.

"Maybe deadly so," Michael quipped, handing her a fresh mug of coffee.

"And a bazillion text messages from Fran." The sight warmed Eu's heart. She'd been missing her bestie so much, and now the laid-back California girl was planning to arrive the next day.

As she finished reading Fran's texts, her phone rang again. It was one of the power company techs letting her know that her power had been restored.

"Oh, thank goodness," she said, after hanging up.

"Power back on?" Michael asked.

"Yep. I'm going to go up there and see if I can talk them out of billing me for the work. Thanks for everything this morning. I owe you," Eu told Michael as she packed up her things.

"Don't mention it. What are neighbors for?" He smiled. "And you can just leave your tackle and chair and minnows down here. I always do and no one touches a thing. It's kind of a fisherperson code."

"Well, that's a relief," Eu replied. "But if you don't mind, I'll take my coffee and return the mug later."

"Not a problem." He raised a hand in farewell as she left.

Things were looking up. She had a mug of coffee, a belly full of baked goods, and her power had been restored. Eu was feeling downright optimistic by the time she crested the hill and stepped out onto the parking lot.

Until she saw Paula Pinson getting out of her car looking hopping mad.

CHAPTER FOURTEEN

"I've got a bone to pick with you, Miss Eugenia," Paula snarled, clearly indignant, when Eu approached.

"Get in line," Eu muttered under her breath. The last thing she needed was a sputtering realtor on her doorstep. "Hi, Paula. What's wrong?" she asked, too exhausted to even work up an innocent act.

"You lied to me, and that's just plain wrong. You weren't working with Sue-Lynn, You just wanted to cozy up and make me talk trash about her because you're trying to save your own skin," Paula seethed.

"I don't even know what you're talking about," Eu said wearily.

"Oh, yes, you do! My little sister is dating Deputy Writman and when we all had pizza last night, I mentioned I had a new client. Imagine my surprise when the deputy warned me about you and said to be careful because you might have murdered your last realtor," she huffed, hands on ample hips.

"Look, first of all, I didn't ask you for any information about Sue-Lynn, you volunteered it. Eagerly, I might add. And second, that's just crazy talk. I didn't murder anyone. If Deputy Dawg can't see past the nose on his face and find the killer, that's his fault, not mine," Eu shot back.

Paula strode toward Eu until they were nearly nose to nose. "Let me tell you something," she snarled, smelling of toothpaste and body spray. "You're the outsider around here, and if it comes down to one of us or you, who do you think they're going to believe? You best watch yourself, and you can forget about working with me. I'm not going to put my reputation on the line for some city girl who comes in and stirs up trouble. You find yourself another realtor."

Eu didn't move an inch, and when Paula made her self-important proclamation, the rage that had been building in her let loose. "I've had just about enough of being called a murderer because I didn't happen to be born and raised here. And you're forgetting something Paula, I don't have a motive. I didn't even know Sue-Lynn, so why on earth would I want to kill her? You, on the other hand, might be tired of always coming in second place behind her, and I've heard jealousy can be a powerful motivator."

Much to her surprise, Paula laughed, but it was a mirthless, smirking laugh that made Eu a bit nervous.

"Here I was thinking you were different because you aren't from around here, but it turns out you might be just plain dumb. I practically spelled out for you who in this town might've killed Sue-Lynn, and it sure as tootin' ain't me. I got a husband who loves me, a nice house, a dog, and a whole lot of other things going for me that Sue-Lynn didn't, so I'm quite happy to be making piles of money and coming in second behind her, thank you very much. Either the scum-sucking boyfriend who was using her for money, or that sad little twit, Helen DeWitt, in her office that let her cheat and pull in a multimillion dollar deal killed her, not me. And to think I actually wanted to help you."

With that, Paula gave her one last glare and got back into her car, leaving the parking lot in a hurry, her tires spinning.

Michael came over the crest of the hill just in time to see Paula's exit.

"You okay?" he asked, jogging over.

Eu stared at Paula's car careening toward the exit. "Methinks the lady doth protest too much."

CHAPTER FIFTEEN

Fran ran from the Uber and wrapped Eu in a giant bear hug. The familiar scent of patchouli and perfume nearly made Eu burst into tears.

"Oh, my gosh it's so good to see you, and it's so beautiful here. I'm loving it already," Fran gushed.

The Uber driver set her bags on the asphalt, told her to have a nice visit, and left, with Fran and Eu barely noticing. Chattering like magpies, they picked up the bags and headed inside.

"This is the most luxurious but comfortable cabin that I've ever seen," Fran marveled as Eu gave her the tour and showed her to her room. "Seriously, your mom had great taste. Have you learned anymore about her?"

Eu shook her head. "Nope, not a thing, other than the fact that she was apparently an amazing fisherman, which blows my mind."

"That's definitely a different twist on what your idea of her has been so far." Fran's brows rose. "But she couldn't have been all bad if she left you this." She held up her hands and turned in a circle.

"Yeah, I figure after I get the murder solved, I'll be able to spend some time trying to figure out more about what my mother was really like and why she left me the cabin."

Fran's eyes went wide. "Speaking of the murder… any news?"

"Well, since the last time we spoke, I met her evil ex-boyfriend who hit on me, then threatened me, and shortly after that, I came back to the cabin to find that my power lines had been cut. The company fixed them yesterday morning," Eu recalled, shaking her head.

"Yikes. Well, after all that mess is resolved, I could totally see you spending some time here. It's amazing. Fresh air, gorgeous scenery…"

Eu shook her head. "No way. I'm an outsider here. No matter how nice some people are, that's how all the other people see me. No thank you, I'll be leaving here as soon as I can."

"It's too bad you couldn't keep it as a summer place and rent it out during the rest of the year," Fran mused, taking in the view.

Eu glanced around at the place her mother had left to her. She shook her head. "No, somehow that doesn't feel right at all. But, hey, you must be starving."

"Way to change the subject," Fran teased. "But yes, I could definitely eat. All I had on the plane were a couple of cookies and like four cups of coffee."

"I could tell." Eu chuckled. "How do fish tacos sound?"

"Like heaven. Let's do it."

The two chattered while they prepared a lunch that had Fran's mouth watering, then sat at the table on the deck to eat.

"Man, this is the life," Fran said, rubbing her full belly and gazing out at the lake.

"I've eaten so much fish, I swear I'm going to start growing gills," Eu said, cracking Fran up.

"Well, at least it'll make you a better swimmer." Fran snickered. "We should go on a nature walk. I need to burn some of these calories off."

"Oh, that's a great idea! I can show you the fishing hole."

Fran gave Eu a look.

"First, I don't fish. Second, I definitely don't want to see the circle of life in action." She made a face.

"Oh, come on, it's actually really cool. We can stop by the clubhouse and the general store along the way," Eu cajoled.

"Fine, but if I see any fish guts, I might just hurl and that would be a waste of a delicious lunch."

"Don't be silly, you don't clean the fish at the fishing hole, I do that down on my dock." Eu grinned.

"I don't even want to know," Fran followed her out the door, muttering.

They stopped by the clubhouse, where Fran insisted upon testing the temperature of the pool by sitting on the side and dunking her feet in, then popped into the general store, where Trixie eyed them curiously while Fran exclaimed about the beautiful minnows swimming in the tank. They bought a couple of giant ice cream sandwiches to eat while they walked down to the fishing hole.

When they entered the building around the fishing hole, Michael and Callie were there. Michael greeted them.

"Afternoon," he said, smiling his hundred watt smile.

"Hi, Michael. This is my best friend, Fran. Fran, this is Michael, and that's Callie." Eu inclined her head toward the older woman, who didn't even glance in their direction.

"Hi! Nice to meet you both," Fran called out.

"You, too," Michael replied.

Callie didn't acknowledge their existence.

"Oh, my gosh, is she deaf?" Fran asked in a stage-whisper.

"No, she's not deaf. She just hates me for some reason," Eu replied in a normal tone of voice.

Michael's brows rose.

Fran nodded, seeming to mull it over. "What did you do?"

Eu rolled her eyes. "I don't think it's something I did, I think it's the mere fact that I exist."

"Are you sure?" Fran persisted. One corner of Callie's mouth lifted slightly. Eu gave Fran a look.

"So, what do you do, tall, dark, and handsome?" Fran asked, turning to Michael. Eu gasped, her eyes going wide.

"I'm a Physics Professor," he replied, chuckling.

"Get outta town, no way!" Fran exclaimed. "If my professors looked like you, I think I would have done a lot better in college."

"Looks are just a random combination of genetic traits, but thank you," Michael replied.

Eu hooked her arm through Fran's. "On that note, we're going to continue on our walk," she announced, dragging Fran toward the door.

"Nice meeting you Michael, Callie."

"You, too." Michael grinned. Callie nodded at Fran.

Eu's mouth dropped open. "Did you put a spell on her or something?" she whispered when they were out of earshot.

"Don't be silly. I don't have any potions with me, and you should really be nicer to her. Her aura is a little muddy, but it's a pleasant color," Fran replied.

"Well, that makes all the difference then." Eu rolled her eyes.

Fran shrugged. "People are just people, whether they're in California or Lake of the Ozarks."

"That's deep," Eu teased.

"You're welcome," Fran said. "Now, take me on the trail by the water and show me that fabulous dock you have. I just don't want to see any fish guts."

After a leisurely walk near the shore, Eu and Fran sat down on the end of the dock, swirling their feet in the chilly lake.

"It really is amazing here, Eu," Fran said, gazing out over the lake.

"Yeah, I know. That's what makes it so hard to decide what I should do."

"Well, I think the first thing you should do is start stepping up your game with the hot professor." Fran nudged Eu with her elbow.

"He is dreamy, isn't he?" Eu said, giggling and blushing.

"Heck yes he is. Work it girl!"

"We'll see about that, but right now, we need to get back to the cabin and have some tea, don't you think?"

"I'm totally good with that," Fran agreed.

They slipped their feet back into their shoes and headed toward the cabin, only to be stopped in their tracks by a horrendous smell as they neared it.

"Holy moly, what is that?" Fran gasped, covering her nose with her hand.

"I have no idea, but I need to find out so I can get rid of it," Eu replied.

"It smells like something died," Fran commented.

The friends exchanged a look.

CHAPTER SIXTEEN

"Someone is really trying to send you a message, Eu," Fran said quietly, her hands wrapped around her mug of tea. "I love this place, but I'm thinking if you stick around her for much longer, you may be the next victim."

"But what possible message could they be trying to send by leaving a bunch of nasty, rotted fish heads and guts in a pile under my deck? It's just so juvenile. Like a prank a kid in junior high might play on someone." Eu sighed.

"Exactly. And what did you think of Sue-Lynn's ex-boyfriend? Don't you think an awful thing like that would be right up his alley? It's not creative, it's gross, and he probably figured it would freak you out," Fran replied. "Sorry I couldn't help you with all that, by the way."

"Oh, don't worry about it. It grossed me out too, but I just couldn't live with that stench. I had to bury it." Eu shuddered at the memory.

"Don't you think it would be better to just lock the door, leave, and never look back?" Fran asked softly, putting her hand over Eu's.

"From a practical standpoint, I can't leave. The deputies told me I have to stick around until I'm officially cleared, and I don't see that happening any time soon, unless I do all the investigating myself."

"Then we need to channel Scooby Doo and figure this mess out, because this is some next level spooky stuff," Fran said.

"Agreed. I feel like either the ex-boyfriend or Paula Pinson did it. Because he's just a bad character no matter who you ask, and she was awfully defensive when she came to see me. I think she just tossed the other agent, Helen DeWitt, from Sue-Lynn's office out there as a distraction," Eu replied.

"But what if she didn't?" Fran asked. "I mean, you were trying to use her without her knowing it. She just happened to make it easy for you. Maybe there's some resentment that had been brewing in the other agent for a long time and it finally just bubbled over for some reason. Maybe we should meet with her."

"You're right. If nothing else, we'd be leaving no stone unturned, and it might even be helpful," Eu agreed. "But it's too late to go over there now. She's probably gone for the day, so we'll do it first thing tomorrow."

A knock sounded at the front door, and they froze, giving each other a look. Fran was the first to take a breath and shake it off. "If it's the ex-boyfriend, I say we tackle him," she whispered with a mischievous grin.

Eu laughed and shook her head, glad that her irreverent bestie had injected some humor into their day yet again. "Alright, let's do this," she said, striding confidently to the door.

"Evening, ladies," Michael said when she opened it. "I have some freshly baked brownies that are still warm, and a pint of double chocolate ice cream that pairs well with them."

He handed an insulated bag and a foil-covered plate to Eu.

"You bake? Holy moly, I wasn't hungry for dinner, but I'll totally eat this," Fran exclaimed, eyeing the plate.

"Would you like to come in and have some with us?" Eu asked.

"I can't. I already had several. Quality control, of course. And I have a kitchen to clean. You two enjoy," Michael replied, turning to go.

Fran lifted the foil and sniffed the brownies, her eyes rolling back in her head.

"Hey, will you marry me, Michael?" she called out as he headed back to his cabin.

He turned and laughed. "I'm not the marrying kind, but thanks for the proposal. I haven't had one in a while."

Eu cracked up and nudged Fran with her elbow. "Girl, you are out of your mind."

"If you play your cards right, you might be the one who changes that hunk's mind about marriage." Fran winked.

Eu pretended to shudder. "No, thank you. I agree with him on that one. I haven't seen a marriage yet that worked out."

"Then be a trend setter."

"Nah, I'm way too busy for that. Right now, I'm not going to think about anything other than eating brownies and ice cream and beating you mercilessly at board games," Eu replied, heading for the kitchen.

"Says you," Fran challenged.

"Oh, man, I needed this." Eu sighed contentedly as she and Fran stashed the board games they'd enjoyed after filling up on brownies and ice cream.

"Yeah, me too," Fran agreed, yawning and stretching. "And now what I need is some serious time cuddled up with those fluffy pillows in the guest room."

"Have a good sleep," Eu said, giving her bestie a hug before she headed down the hall.

Tired, but her mind whirling with too many thoughts to even think about going to sleep, Eu played games on her phone until she couldn't keep her eyes open.

At least this time, when she finally fell asleep, it was a deep restful sleep. It was amazing how much safer she felt with Fran in the house.

CHAPTER SEVENTEEN

Yawning and stretching, Eu glanced out the window at the lake and smiled. Her peaceful morning was shattered however, when she heard a noise. She texted Fran to see if it was her, but heard her phone buzzing gently on the nightstand on the other side of her bed.

Grabbing a decorative fishing pole from its shelf over a mirror, Eu slipped her phone into the pocket of her pajama bottoms and gripped the pole like a baseball bat. She tried to silently open her door, wincing when the doorknob made an audible click.

Moving out into the hall, she glanced at the open bathroom door. No Fran. She peered into the guest room and saw nothing on the bed but an empty tangle of blankets. Moving further down the hall, she smelled the heavenly scent of freshly brewed coffee, and she relaxed a bit. An intruder wouldn't take the time to make coffee while they rummaged through possessions.

"Good morning, sunshine," Fran said, with her characteristic grin. "And just what on earth do you intend to do with that?" She gazed at the decorative fishing pole that Eu currently had raised overhead.

"Well, if you had been a stone-cold killer, I was going to defend myself." Eu laughed, relieved. She leaned the pole against the wall.

"As far as I know, killers don't make their victims coffee and fix them brownies. We're all set up for breakfast on the deck, sleepyhead. Go get settled out there. I was about to start without you. I thought you were going to sleep forever."

"I didn't get to sleep quite as early as you did, and with all the weirdness going on right now, I'm actually surprised I slept at all."

"It's the fresh air, it'll make you sleep whether you want to or not. I figured we needed sustenance before we went to face off with a realtor who might be a killer," Fran replied, holding up a massive brownie, then taking a bite from it. "Oh, that man is talented," she murmured, savoring the bite.

"Agreed. You should taste his cinnamon rolls."

"Do tell." Fran batted her eyes.

"Oh, stop. He took pity on me when I first got here. We had coffee and cinnamon rolls on his front porch. He was just being neighborly."

"Why can't I have a neighbor like that?" Fran asked, with a mock pout.

They had a leisurely breakfast, appreciating every bite of brownie and sip of coffee, then took their dishes inside and went to their rooms to get ready to meet Helen DeWitt.

"Hey, do you know where my phone is? I can't find it anywhere," Fran asked when they regrouped in the living room before heading out. She had apparently tousled her California beach hair when she got out of the shower and was wearing an outfit that resembled something that Stevie Nicks might wear on a summer holiday.

Eu reached into the pocket of her denim shorts and pulled out the phone. "Here you go. You must've left it on the nightstand yesterday. Nice outfit by the way. I'm sure you'll blend in really well with the locals." She grinned.

"Take notes. If you're going to land the hot professor, you need to dress it up a bit. The fish can't bite if there's no bait on the hook." Fran struck a dramatic pose, hand on hip, with pouty lips.

Eu could feel herself blushing scarlet. "Well, fortunately, I'm not trying to land anyone. I just want to get this case solved and figure out how to sell the cabin without leaving anyone in the lurch."

Helen DeWitt was a plump and innocent-looking woman who reminded Eu of the school secretary from Ferris Bueller. After she seated Eu and Fran in her office, with cups of cocoa in front of each of them, she gave them a sweet smile and asked how she could help them.

Eu opened her mouth to speak, and the desk phone rang. Helen gave it an annoyed look.

"I'm sorry, they know I'm not to be disturbed when I have clients in my office so it must be important," she said, picking up the receiver.

"Hello, this is Helen," she said, the smile on her face seeming strained before it disappeared altogether. "This is not the time…" Eu heard her say before she turned away from the desk, speaking quietly, but ferociously into the phone. Eu and Fran exchanged a look.

Fran cupped a hand beside her mouth and leaned toward Eu. "I'm glad I'm not the one on the other end of the line," she whispered.

Eu raised her eyebrows and nodded. "Uh, should we…" Eu inclined her head toward the door.

Helen shook her head and held up one finger. She said her goodbyes to whoever she'd been talking to and hung up the phone.

"I'm so sorry about that. Now, how can I help you two?"

"I'm looking into potentially selling a property, but I'm not sure yet, so I was just wondering if you could work up an overview of the market here for me," Eu said.

"Oh, sure, hon. I'd be happy to."

"That's great. I'll drop by in a few days and pick it up, then I can give you a call when I'm ready to list."

"Sounds good to me." Helen beamed.

"Her former realtor was murdered," Fran said.

"Oh, dear, I'm so sorry. You were working with Sue-Lynn?" Helen's voice wavered.

Eu nodded.

"What a shame. She and I might not have seen eye to eye on business matters, but she was a good person who never hurt anyone. Bless her heart. Well, don't you worry, I'll take good care of you. It's the least I can do," Helen said.

Eu thanked her again and they left. When they got on the scooter, Fran was frowning.

"What did you think?" Eu asked.

"I'm confused," Fran admitted with a shrug.

"Oh? Why?"

"Because Helen acted really suspiciously, like she was a total phony, smiling at us then tearing someone to pieces on the phone, but she had a really nice aura."

"Well, unfortunately, we have to have something a bit more concrete than a nice aura to go on," Eu said ruefully.

When they pulled up to the cabin, Paula Pinson was parked out front.

"Oh, great, get ready for battle," Eu murmured.

Paula got out of her car, dressed like a real estate professional, right down to her chic but sensible kitten heels. Her tasteful accessories sparkled in the morning sun.

"Hello, Eugenia. Sorry to just drop in on you like this, but I want to apologize for my behavior the last time we met. I've been real tense these past couple of weeks because I can't help but wonder if Sue-Lynn was killed because someone doesn't like realtors or something. I could be next. I mean, it's always a little nerve-wracking to go into vacant listings, but now I'm even carrying pepper spray in my purse, just in case."

"That's understandable. I never even considered it might've been some sort of weird crusade against realtors, or maybe even just a random thing. I guess that happens sometimes. Seems like a small town would be an odd place to choose to do it, but who knows what's in the mind of someone who would do something like that," Eu replied, carefully watching Paula for a reaction.

"Yeah. I've probably been way too worried about the whole mess, but I guess that's what I get for watching re-runs of CSI." Paula attempted a smile that didn't quite work. "So anyhoo, sorry again for acting like a horse's heinie."

"No worries. I'm sure everyone around here is a bit rattled," Eu replied, also faking a smile.

Paula got into her car and left, giving a jaunty wave as she went.

"Well, that was unexpected," Fran said as they headed toward the house.

"Yeah, and full of bunk," Eu replied.

"What do you mean?" Fran frowned.

"Murders are usually personal. The victim and the killer know each other just about every time, except when it's a serial killer, and as far as I know, no one else has died, so this doesn't fit the pattern of a serial killer," Eu mused.

"You know way too much about all this stuff." Fran shuddered.

"Occupational hazard." Eu sighed. "It's weird though that Paula's story about why she's been stressed was pretty lame, but her apology seemed real. It's hard to pull off an apology if you're not sincere about it."

"Maybe she's a well-mannered cold-blooded killer."

"You're hilarious. But no, I really don't get a killer vibe from her anymore. I think she's genuinely scared, even if she's lying about why. And I didn't get killer vibes from Helen either," Eu thought aloud. "So that just leaves…"

"The ex-boyfriend," Fran supplied. "Which is what you've thought since the beginning. So now what do we do? How do we smoke him out?"

"We go get ourselves some epic barbeque," Eu replied with a sly smile.

"Huh?"

"There's a server at a local barbeque joint who gave me info about the boyfriend when I first started poking into things. Maybe she'll give me more info now."

"If solving a crime involves partaking in fantastic barbeque, I will make that sacrifice. I'm just that kind of friend." Fran grinned.

"Somehow I knew you were."

CHAPTER EIGHTEEN

"Hey, new girl. How are you doing?" the server at the barbeque joint asked when Eu and Fran came in.

"I'm great, thanks. How are you?"

"I can't complain." The server shrugged. "Ain't nobody would listen if I did." She chuckled. "Did you ever go check out that boat tour?"

"No, I haven't gotten that far yet," Eu replied truthfully.

"Probably just as well, but you missed your chance anyhow. They're closed for the off-season now."

Eu and Fran exchanged an excited glance.

"Come on over with me. I'll give you two the best table in the house."

They took a seat by a wall of windows that had a fantastic view of the lake.

"Our special today is the sampler plate, and if y'all want to split it, there's plenty of food for two."

"Sounds good to me," Fran said. "How about you?"

Eu nodded. "Sounds great, thanks."

After the server left, Fran leaned across the table. "Oh, my gosh, if they're closed down for the season, we can walk down there and snoop around," she whispered.

"Absolutely. That's totally what I was thinking," Eu agreed.

The food arrived heaped on a platter and Eu's stomach rumbled.

"Oh my," Fran said, her eyes wide.

"Challenge accepted," Eu said, grinning.

There was succulent sliced brisket, tender baby back ribs, perfectly cooked and seasoned barbecued chicken, spicy polish sausage, and all the fixings, including smoky baked beans, cool crispy coleslaw, and moist, warm, buttery cornbread with honey.

"Why did you wait so long to take me here?" Fran demanded, savoring every bite. "There's no way we're going to finish this."

"We'll take the rest home," Eu said, glad that Fran was enjoying herself.

They ate. And ate. And ate.

After using wet wipes to clean their hands, the two friends went to the scooter and secured the food in one of the saddlebags.

"I think to walk off all of that food, we should head to the waterfront, don't you?" Fran asked, nodding at the sign that advertised the lake cruise.

"You read my mind," Eu agreed. "Let's go between the buildings to get to the shore and then head over there."

They made their way down to the footpath near the lake and started toward the large dock where Beau's boat was moored. When the path ended, they climbed over fallen trees and rocks to get to the dock. Just back from the shore, a landing that was attached to the dock, had a shack on it that served as the office for the business and ticket sales.

They tried the doorknob, which was locked, then peered in the windows.

"Dark in there," Fran commented.

"Yep, but by the looks of it, there isn't much to see there anyway. Let's go check out the boat," Eu replied.

"What if someone sees us?" Fran whispered, gripping Eu's arm.

Eu made a show of looking in every direction. "Like who? It's off-season, no one will be around here. Besides, if anyone sees us, we can just say we were looking for someone to see if they'd make an exception and give us a tour." She shrugged.

"Is this what you learned from pretending to be a reporter? Who even are you right now?" Fran said, shaking her head.

"You could wait here," Eu replied.

"And miss out on the fun? Not on your life," Fran said with a mischievous grin.

They strode down the dock toward the boat as if it was the most normal thing in the world, and when they were close enough to jump across the gap between the dock and the boat, they did.

"Welp, here we are trespassing," Fran murmured. "I guess it's all downhill from here."

"Sound carries across water, you know," Eu whispered.

Fran took the hint and stayed quiet but made a face at her bestie.

They wandered around the outside decks of the boat, since the doors to get inside were locked, and suddenly Eu stopped and nudged Fran with her elbow, an excited smile on her face. Trapped between what looked like a pair of tall oxygen tanks was a wallet.

"Do you have a tissue?" Eu whispered.

Fran dug in her purse and handed over a tissue without comment. Eu carefully wrapped her fingers in it and grabbed the wallet, prying it free. It flopped open, showing a familiar object, one of Sue-Lynn's business cards. Eu looked at Fran, brows raised. Fran nodded and held her purse open. Eu dropped the wallet into the purse.

They both heard a thunk that sounded like it came from the dock and froze.

"Let's get out of here," Eu said, pushing Fran toward the exit.

As they rounded the corner and hurried toward the back of the boat, Eu stopped so fast that Fran ran into the back of her. Beau Garet was standing on the dock right in front of the only exit.

"Y'all know that trespassing is against the law, right?" he drawled, switching a toothpick from one corner of his mouth to the other. "But then again, there ain't no need to bring the law into it. I like to take care of things my way."

He hopped across, onto the deck of the boat and leaned against the sidewall, staring at them like a predator.

"Like you did with Sue-Lynn?" Eu shot back, feeling Fran poke her in the ribs.

"You just ain't got no sense at all, do ya, girl?" Beau growled, taking a step toward them, fists clenched at his sides.

"Well, there you are!" a loud cheery voice called out.

Michael.

He had a sack of something in one hand and waved with the other. "You guys all good?" he asked, trotting down to the dock and heading toward them.

Eu had never been happier to see someone in her life. She waved and smiled. "Yep, we were just leaving."

When Beau turned to see who had interrupted whatever plans he'd had for them, Eu brushed past him and leaped to the dock, dragging Fran behind her. They dashed over to Michael and Eu had to restrain herself from giving him the biggest bear hug he'd ever had.

"Thank you," she whispered.

Michael lifted a hand and waved to Beau. "Have a good evening," he called out, as though he hadn't a care in the world. Beau grimaced and raised a hand in reply. Apparently good ole southern hospitality had been ingrained in him at some point, even though it hadn't stopped him from committing murder.

Once they were out of sight, Eu drew in a shaky breath and let it out in a long sigh.

Michael stopped and faced them. "Okay, ladies. Wanna tell me what you were thinking going down there?"

"I was thinking that Beau Garet is the one who killed Sue-Lynn, and his behavior just now makes me think that I was right," Eu replied.

"Yeah, we even found a wallet that had Sue-Lynn's business card in it on the boat," Fran added.

Eu gave her a look.

"Do tell." Michael quirked an eyebrow at them. "And what exactly did you do with the wallet?" he asked, folding his arms.

"We…uh… we put it in my purse," Fran mumbled.

Michael closed his eyes for a moment, then opened them and shook his head. "You know you have to give it to the sheriff immediately, right?"

"But if we do that, it's going to look like Eu is trying to plant evidence," Fran protested.

"And if you don't do that, she may actually be withholding evidence," Michael replied gravely. "You need to turn it in and tell the truth about how you obtained it. Honesty is always the best policy."

"He's right. I don't want to do it either, but he's right." Eu sighed.

CHAPTER NINETEEN

Eu was relieved that, of the two deputies she'd tangled with, Carter, the better of the two, was the one who sat her down in a conference room to talk to her and Fran.

She explained what happened and braced herself for his reaction.

Carter shook his head. "Do you have any idea how badly you may have just complicated this investigation?" he asked. "Not to mention the fact that, whether your 'hunch' was correct or not, you may have put yourself in danger. I don't know what things are like where you come from, but around here, you don't just trespass and walk around on other folks' property."

Eu and Fran merely stared at him. It went against their grain that he chose to chew them out for trespassing rather than arresting Beau Garet for his threats.

"Alright, hand it over," he said.

"We didn't touch it. We used a tissue to pick it up," Eu said. Fran opened her purse and handed Eu another tissue. She grabbed the wallet with it and dropped it on the table in front of Carter, who put on a nitrile glove, picked up the wallet, and put it in an evidence bag.

"You're welcome," Fran said, smiling sweetly. Carter glanced at her, then turned his attention to Eu.

"Y'all need to leave this investigation up to us. If I find out you've been sniffing around Beau Garet or anyone else, I won't have any problem at all throwing you in lockup for obstruction, are we clear on that, ladies?"

"Wow, aren't you even the least bit grateful that we helped you?" Fran asked.

Carter flushed red from the base of his neck to the tips of his ears. "Little lady, if we needed your help, we would have asked for it. There ain't nothin' to be gained from some city girl and her hippie friend poking their noses into places that they ain't got no business being in. And you..." he stared Fran down, "...ought to stay around town for a while, now that you might be an accessory after the fact."

"Oh, sweetie, you couldn't blast me out of here with dynamite since my friend has been wrongly accused and you've obviously been barking up the wrong tree," Fran replied, her eyes flashing fire.

Carter got up, went to the door, opened it, and stood back so that they had a clear path out.

"That went well," Eu said dryly. "How on earth are you going to be able to stay away from the store longer? You have to be there on a daily basis and the way things are going here, this stupid crime may never be solved."

"I'll figure something out now that we both have to clear our names." Fran shrugged.

"And what came over you? I've never seen anything break through your zen like this. You actually looked angry," Eu marveled.

"No, not angry. Assertive." Fran grinned, back to normal.

Eu pulled into her parking spot and stopped short when she looked at the porch. Fran followed her gaze.

"What now?" Eu said wearily, spotting a package on the porch.

"Oh, geez…what if it's another message that someone is sending?" Fran murmured, getting their barbeque leftovers out of the saddlebag.

They approached slowly and Eu saw the package was a gift-wrapped box.

"Maybe it's from the professor?" Fran guessed.

"But what if it isn't?" Eu replied, chewing on her bottom lip.

"Should we unwrap it?" Fran wondered.

"I'm not even sure if we should move it," Eu said, not getting too close to the package.

"It's safe," Michael called out, on his way to the fishing hole. "I saw Kyle Bresden drop it off for you."

"Well, isn't it nice that even out here in the sticks there's a neighborhood watch program." Fran chuckled.

Eu grinned, despite herself. "Thanks, Michael," she called out and waved.

He waved back and continued on his way. Eu picked up the box and something inside rattled a bit.

"Okay, now who is Kyle Bresden?" Fran asked, as they went inside. "You've never mentioned him and here he is giving you a present. Is he cuter than Michael?"

"No way, not even close," Eu protested, then blushed. "He's a developer who thinks he's way hotter than he is. Way too slick for my taste."

"It'd be hard to beat Michael, who always seems to come to the rescue right when you need him most," Fran teased, making Eu blush harder. "Open the thing already, my curiosity is killing me!"

Eu unwrapped a sectioned clear plastic box that was filled with high-end fishing lures. There was a note attached. It was an apology from Kyle for putting his foot in his mouth and being a clod, followed by an invitation to dinner. He included his phone number and a suggestion that she text him.

"Well, you might be gaga over the professor, but it seems that this guy certainly has the hots for you,"

Fran mused. "How he thinks he'd win your heart with a bunch of fake fish with hooks sticking out of them is beyond me, though. Are you going to take him up on his offer?"

"Definitely not. I don't have the time or the inclination," Eu replied.

"But if he's a developer, don't you think he might know something about Sue-Lynn, or even Beau?"

Eu stared at her friend. "I never thought about that. Realtors and developers do tend to work together quite a bit."

"Then maybe you should go to dinner with him. It's a free meal and you might just learn something important about the case," Fran pointed out.

"Ick, but okay. That makes sense. I'll text him."

A reply to Eu's text popped up within moments. Kyle sent her the name of a restaurant and asked her to meet him there.

"What are you going to wear?" Fran asked.

Eu blinked at her.

"No, you are not wearing jean shorts to dinner, whether you dislike this guy or not," Fran insisted. "Come with me. I'll loan you something presentable, but comfortable," she promised.

"I don't want to go," Eu grumbled.

"Yes, but since you agreed to, you need an outfit."

"Fine." Eu sighed and trudged down the hall. At least the lures were nice.

CHAPTER TWENTY

"You look amazing," Fran gushed when Eu came out of her room.

"I look like Aerosmith and Helen Reddy had a baby." Eu rolled her eyes, smoothing down the sides of the harem pants that Fran had provided.

"I hadn't thought of that, but yes, I see it, and I like it." Fran nodded her approval. "At least you got Steven Tyler's hair."

Eu hugged her bestie and went out the door, a strange worry gnawing at her midsection. It wasn't just date nerves. While it was true that she hadn't been on an actual date in quite some time, the feeling in the pit of her stomach stemmed from something more than that. Something she couldn't quite put her finger on.

Eu started up the scooter and hesitated before leaving the parking lot. She saw Fran in the front window, shooing her away and laughed, trying to shake off her trepidation. She hit the gas and headed out of the resort, not even making it a mile before the feelings gnawing at her stomach became too strong to ignore. She looked for a place to pull off of the road, and once she did, she rolled the scooter into the tree line, hiding it behind a clump of bushes.

Taking out her phone, Eu did a couple of quick searches that confirmed her suspicions. Her gut told her that she was right, so she had to follow it. Using a trail through the woods that wreaked havoc on her strappy sandals and Fran's harem pants, Eu headed back toward her cabin as quickly as she could, her progress hampered by the waning light and an outfit that definitely wasn't meant for hiking in the woods.

When she came to the far side of the marina that was across the resort peninsula from the fishing hole, she wound her way through the woods and followed the edge of the lake until she came to Michael's cabin.

Making sure she wouldn't be seen, she darted to the side of his cabin and knocked on the kitchen window.

He turned quickly from the stove, switched off the burner and hurried to the window, where he spotted Eu. She beckoned to him to come outside and put a finger to her lips. Sound carried easily among the cabins because of the water, and she wasn't taking any chances.

Michael wiped his hands on a kitchen towel and hurried toward the door. Eu crouched down between his cabin and a clump of bushes to wait for him, sending up a plea to the skies that nothing creepy and crawly with multiple legs would drop down on her.

"What's going on?" Michael whispered, crouching down near the bushes and pretending to examine a branch.

"I can't explain how, but I know who the killer is. Call the sheriff and tell them to come to my cabin," Eu replied.

"Wait, is the killer there now? You aren't thinking of going over there are you? You should wait for the sheriff," Michael said, his eyes darting toward Eu's cabin.

Eu's eyes pleaded with him. "Michael, I can't. Fran is in there. I've got to go do something. I would never forgive myself if..." Her words cut off as a lump formed in her throat.

"Okay, okay, I get it, but at least let me come with you. There's safety in numbers."

Eu shook her head. "I know that, but it'll be way easier for me to sneak in alone than for two of us to try and sneak in. Please, just call the sheriff and stay here so no one else gets hurt because of me."

"Fine, but if it takes them more than a few minutes to get here, I'll be breaking down your door."

"If it takes them more than a few minutes to get here, I'll want you to break down my door," Eu agreed.

"Fair enough. Be careful," Michael reminded her. "You're dealing with someone who already killed once. They have nothing left to lose."

Eu nodded. "One last thing. Can I borrow your step ladder?" she asked.

"Of course." Michael hurried off to get it, already on the phone with the sheriff's department.

He handed it to Eu in a matter of seconds and she slipped from behind the bushes, headed toward her cabin. She paused underneath her kitchen window when she heard voices raised in anger coming from inside.

Her legs and lungs burning with exertion, Eu carefully unfolded the step ladder and positioned it beneath the lowest part of her deck, thanking her lucky stars that the property had been built on a slope that led down to the lake. Once the ladder was positioned, she snuck over to her fish cleaning station near the dock and grabbed her sharpest filet knife.

After ascending the step ladder with the knife clenched in her fist, Eu crawled up onto the deck, creeping behind and between patio furniture so that she couldn't be seen. Moving closer and closer to the sliding door, she saw Fran and the killer arguing in the kitchen. Thankfully his back was to the slider, so if Fran had forgotten to lock it like she usually did, Eu could sneak in and surprise him.

She edged closer to the slider and placed her fingers on the strip of metal that stood between her and her best friend. Holding her breath, Eu tugged. Relief flooded through her when the door gave way, sliding back toward her a tiny bit.

It was now or never.

Using every bit of the strength and adrenaline that she had within her, Eu slid the door open, slipped through and took a running jump, landing on the killer's back. Moving fast, she wrapped her legs around his waist, locking her feet at the ankles, and threw her left arm around his neck, placing the cool, sharp blade at his throat with her right hand before he even had a chance to react.

"Don't move. I've known how to use a filet knife since I was a kid and I won't hesitate," she threatened through gritted teeth, her breath heaving in and out in sharp little puffs.

The color had drained from Fran's face.

"Fran, get the zip ties from the junk drawer and secure his wrists and ankles," Eu ordered, her left arm shaking with exertion.

Fran turned to get the zip ties, and the killer tried to flip Eu over his head, which made the knife sink into his skin just a tiny bit.

He howled with pain, but stopped resisting, just as two deputies slammed Eu's front door open.

CHAPTER TWENTY-ONE

The first two deputies were followed by two more deputies. They filed in, weapons drawn. Two of them moved in front of the slider, the other two advanced slowly, positioning themselves between the killer and the front door.

"It's about time you showed up," the killer bellowed. "Get this madwoman who's trying to slit my throat off of me."

"If I was trying to slit your throat, you'd be on the floor by now," Eu hissed, her teeth clenched.

"Alright now, let's just calm down," Carter said, holstering his weapon and holding up his hands. "Eugenia, you need to come on down from there."

"Are you kidding me right now? You believe him? Let me just tell you what this worthless piece of garbage has done. He was supporting Beau Garet's business after Sue-Lynn dumped him and he killed Sue-Lynn because the deal that she snatched away from Helen DeWitt she also snatched out from under him. He would have developed half the lakefront in this county if it weren't for Sue-Lynn selling it while he was trying to sweet-talk Helen into giving him a better price," Eu raged, not budging an inch.

Carter nodded. "Yeah, we know. His fingerprints were also all over the utility box after your lines had been cut. Pretty sure they're going to be on the sticks of dynamite that we just found tucked up near your foundation too," he replied. "Now, nice and easy, come on down."

"Oh," Eu said, stunned at the thought of her cabin being blown to bits.

As she released her hold and her feet dropped down to the floor, Kyle Bresden lunged for the knife. Darting to the side, Eu snatched it out of his reach and plunged it squarely through the rear pocket of Kyle's jeans. Fran gasped and one of the deputies by the door lunged forward to remove the knife before Kyle could get to it.

Moaning in pain, the killer submitted to being handcuffed, blood darkening the back of his pants.

"Get him outside and call medical transport, I don't want that mess in the back of my cruiser," Carter told Writman.

"You just stabbed a man in the heinie," Fran murmured, staring wide-eyed at Eu.

"That's funny…I didn't see nothin' like that happen, did y'all?" Carter asked the other deputies, giving them a meaningful look. They all shook their heads.

"No, sir, didn't see nothin' of the sort," one replied. "Looked to me like he had that there knife in his hand and fell on the dang thing."

"I think we're done here, then." Carter dismissed the deputies, lingering until they were gone. "You ladies can come into the station in the morning to give your statement." He stared hard at Eu. "You and I are gonna talk."

She nodded and he left. Fran ran over and wrapped her fierce little bestie in a bear hug.

"You are seriously the bravest person I've ever known," Fran said, trembling a bit.

"Nah, I've just been waiting my whole life to stab someone in the tuckus." Eu laughed, finally able to let go of the fear and stress she'd been carrying.

They heard a knock at the door.

"Seriously? Eu shook her head. "What now?"

She opened the door and noted that Michael's handsome face had never been so dear.

"Hey, ladies, I brought chocolate chip cookies and bourbon. Thought they might come in handy."

CHAPTER TWENTY-TWO

After what had been her absolute best night's sleep in the Ozarks, Eu woke up to see an insulated tumbler of coffee on her nightstand with a note from Fran on it that simply said, 'Gone fishing.'

"Wait… Fran doesn't fish. What's that girl up to now?" Eu giggled and climbed out of bed.

She dressed quickly, ate a couple of cookies, washing them down with sips of coffee, grabbed her fishing gear and headed for the fishing hole, where she discovered Fran, sitting cross-legged next to Callie, chattering away like an old friend.

Callie's expression changed at the sight of Eu, seeming to shut down.

"Thanks for the coffee," Eu said, still wondering what Fran had been up to. "You're up early."

"Well, since I'm leaving tomorrow, I figured I should probably make the most of today," Fran replied, standing up and dusting off the seat of her shorts. She moved to a camp stool that was next to Eu's chair and sat on it.

The three of them sat in silence for a while after Eu dropped her line into the fishing hole. Callie got a bite and reeled in a nice sized catfish. Fran grabbed a net and scooped it up for her, beaming when the big fish hit the deck, squirming in the net. Callie nodded to her, one corner tilting upward into what looked like a grateful half-smile.

Callie took the catfish off of the hook, put it in her basket and trundled toward the door without a word.

"Your new best buddy?" Eu said lightly after Callie was out of earshot.

Fran's expression was somber. "It's not about you, it's about your mom."

Eu's brows rose. "Huh?"

"I haven't gotten the entire story, but apparently something happened between Callie and your mom. You need to use those detective skills of yours to figure out what happened, because Callie isn't a bad person. I swear to you, she isn't," Fran replied.

Eu nodded, her mind racing. "Well, I'm planning on staying here for a while, so it's not like I won't have the time."

"How long are you planning to stay?" Fran asked.

"Until I figure out what I'm going to do. The articles I've turned in have paid pretty well, so I'll at least be able to survive until I make a decision."

"Yeah, I get that. But at some point, maybe after you get to know more about your mom, it'll probably be a healthy idea for you to move on."

Eu nodded, unsure as to how she felt about that.

They sat in companionable silence for a while, with Eu moving her pole around to various locations trying to find the fish.

"I think they're napping," Fran said, after watching Eu drop her line in for the umpteenth time.

"I think you're right," Eu said, chuckling. "How about, since it's your last day here, we go into town and have lunch, then we can go to one of the souvenir shops that's still open. I brought California clothes here and it's starting to get chilly in the mornings, so I'll need some sweatshirts."

"Sounds like fun. Let's do it."

Eu reeled in her line and left her pole, chair, and tackle box behind. Michael had been right about the fisherman code. No one had touched anything of hers that she'd left behind and that made it much easier to go back and forth from the cabin to the fishing hole.

Fran looked pensive as they trudged up the hill toward the cabin to get ready for lunch.

"Everything okay?" Eu asked.

Fran sighed. "Yeah, I'm just worried about you, I guess."

"Worried about me? Why?" Eu asked. "The killer has been caught, it's all good now."

"No, it's not that. Like you said, it's getting colder here and when all the shops close up, it could be really hard to find food and basic necessities."

Eu smiled. "I'll be okay. The grocery stores here stay open year round."

"And what are you going to do, take the scooter to the store in a snowstorm? You don't even have any winter clothes."

"I know. I'll buy a couple more sweatshirts today, and if I'm still here during the winter, there's a thrift store in town. I'll be fine, I promise. I don't have many survival skills, but I know how to shop, even when I'm somewhere where Amazon doesn't deliver," Eu assured Fran, draping an arm around her shoulders and giving her a quick squeeze. "It's still a little early yet for lunch, how about we take a walk around the resort to stretch our legs before we go?" she suggested.

"I'm up for it." Fran smiled, but Eu could still see the concern in her eyes.

They walked all the way through the complex, to the top of the hill, waved to Trixie as they passed by the general store, and headed back down to the cabin to freshen up. Michael was on his front porch, drinking coffee and concentrating on his phone when they reached his cabin.

"Morning!" he greeted them. "This is your last day, isn't it, Fran?" he asked.

"Yep, I'm headed out bright and early tomorrow."

"Well, if I don't see you before then, have a safe trip. I enjoyed meeting you."

"Same." Fran smiled. "But I will say that I think my best friend is a little naïve."

Eu's heart leapt to her throat, and she gave Fran a look that warned her not to say anything to Michael about Eu's crush on him.

"Really? She seems pretty savvy to me." He shrugged.

"She's thinking she might stay here through the winter, and I've told her it's crazy to even consider it," Fran said, giving Eu a 'please forgive me, it's all out of love' look.

"Wow. That's maybe not the best course of action," Michael said carefully. "As far as I know, nobody but Callie stays here through the winter. Sometimes the roads make it hard to get anywhere."

"We'll cross that bridge when we come to it, I guess," Eu said, a bit too brightly. "But we should head out. We're going to lunch and souvenir shopping today."

"Well, you ladies have fun. And take care, Fran."

"Thanks. You too," she replied.

"You threw me under the bus," Eu accused lightly as they continued their walk.

"I was hoping maybe if we ganged up on you, you'd change your mind," Fran confessed.

"I haven't even made up my mind yet. Winter is a while away, so I have time to think and decide my next steps," Eu said, linking her arm through Fran's. "For now, let's just enjoy the last seconds of your visit."

"I'm going to miss you," Fran said, resting her head on Eu's shoulder for a moment.

"Me too," Eu replied, a lump forming in her throat.

"So, what are we going to do after lunch and shopping?" Fran asked, wiping at her eyes.

"How about a fish fry and movie night?" Eu suggested. "We can get some popcorn and candy at the general store and hang out in our jammies like we did at the apartment."

"Sounds perfect," Fran agreed. "That apartment has been so quiet since you've been here."

"I miss it. I also miss the convenience of coffee bistros within walking distance. And the beach. And patio parties with our friends," Eu mused. "But there's some kind of magnetic pull to this place that just keeps reeling me in."

"Nice fish metaphor," Fran teased. "But I think once you've figured out more about your mom it'll be easier to get closure and go back to your life."

"Maybe. Or maybe I'll discover a whole new life. Who knows?"

CHAPTER TWENTY-THREE

After an evening of laughter and fun, Eu had another wonderful sleep, but when she opened her eyes and checked the time, a fierce sadness clutched at her heart. Fran would be leaving in a couple of hours, and the cabin would go back to being a quiet place without the joy and mirth that always seemed to bubble over in her best friend.

"We had a pretty great time here, all things considered," Fran said as they sipped coffee, curled up on the living room couches. "So, what are you going to do after I leave?"

"I'll be working on articles non-stop. They pay well, and I think it'll be fun to disappear into research for a while. Aside from investigating a murder and sending in a handful of articles, I've basically felt like I'm on vacation, so it's time to step up my productivity a bit," Eu replied, actually looking forward to diving into her new assignments.

"Enjoying not having a boss, huh?" Fran grinned.

"Heck yes. It turns out I do much better work when I don't have someone breathing down my neck or giving me pointless tasks to do."

"Imagine that." Fran laughed softly. "Oh, I almost forgot to tell you! I was looking through some of the paperback books your mom left in the guest room, and something fell out of one of them." She dug in her pocket and pulled out a frayed satin ribbon that had clearly once been red, but which had faded to a soft pink around the edges.

Eu's eyes went wide, and she gasped. "How did she get this?" she murmured, opening her hand so Fran could place it delicately on her palm.

"Is there something special about it?" Fran asked, moving closer to gaze at the simple ribbon.

Eu looked up at her with unshed tears shimmering in her eyes and nodded. "It's one of the hair ties that I used to wear when I was little. I've always loved red. I have pictures in my photo album of me wearing two ribbons like this in my ponytails. The matching one is in my jewelry box at home."

"Wow. She kept that all these years and left it in her special retreat place," Fran said.

Eu shook her head. "I don't know how she would have it, or why she would have kept it."

"There's probably more to your mom than you realize," Fran said softly. "Maybe you should use your investigative reporter skills to look into that."

Eu nodded. "Yeah, I will."

A honk sounded from outside and the friends exchanged a sad look. It was time.

Fran checked her phone to confirm. "That's my Uber."

After moving her luggage outside, they clung to each other, not ashamed of their tears, until finally a sigh from the driver prompted Fran to pull back. They said their final goodbyes and Eu stood on her porch until the Uber car was out of sight.

Michael approached just as she was about to go inside. "You okay?" he asked as Eu wiped her cheeks.

"I will be," she said, smiling wanly. "Before she left, Fran said there may be more to my mother than I realize, and that I should do some digging to find out."

Michael nodded. "From what I've seen, I'd say she's probably right. You've had a heck of a time here so far. How are you holding up?"

Eu laughed softly. "I'm pretty good now that I'm not a murder suspect, and at least I got some really good lures out of the whole mess."

"Are you seriously considering staying through the winter?" Michael asked.

"I guess I'll stay as long as it takes."

"As long as it takes for what?"

Eu thought for a moment. "As long as it takes to figure out what kind of person my mother was and what kind of person I am, I guess."

Michael smiled – that gorgeous smile that gave him dimples and crinkled the corners of his eyes. "I think you'll likely be pleasantly surprised on both counts."

***

If you enjoyed Lured By Murder, check out Casting Doubt, book 2 in the Fish Camp Cozy Mystery series.

ALSO BY SUMMER PRESCOTT

Check out all the books in Summer Prescott's catalog!

Summer Prescott Book Catalog

AUTHOR'S NOTE

I'd love to hear your thoughts on my books, the storylines, and anything else that you'd like to comment on—reader feedback is very important to me. My contact information, along with some other helpful links, is listed on the next page. If you'd like to be on my list of "folks to contact" with updates, release and sales notifications, etc.… just shoot me an email and let me know. Thanks for reading!

Also…

… if you're looking for more great reads, Summer Prescott Books publishes several popular series by outstanding Cozy Mystery authors.

CONTACT SUMMER PRESCOTT BOOKS PUBLISHING

Twitter: @summerprescott1

Bookbub: https://www.bookbub.com/authors/summer-prescott

Blog and Book Catalog: http://summerprescottbooks.com

Email: summer.prescott.cozies@gmail.com

YouTube: https://www.youtube.com/channel/UCngKNUkDdWuQ5k7-Vkfrp6A

And…be sure to check out the Summer Prescott Cozy Mysteries fan page and Summer Prescott Books Publishing Page on Facebook – let's be friends!

CONTACT SUMMER PRESCOTT BOOKS PUBLISHING

To download a free book, and sign up for our fun and exciting newsletter, which will give you opportunities to win prizes and swag, enter contests, and be the first to know about New Releases, click here: http://summerprescottbooks.com

Printed in Great Britain
by Amazon